OUR
GEN

ALSO BY DIANE McKINNEY-WHETSTONE

OUR
GEN

A Novel

Diane McKinney-Whetstone

AMISTAD

An Imprint of HarperCollins*Publishers*

OUR GEN. Copyright © 2022 by Diane McKinney-Whetstone. All rights reserved. Printed in the United States of America. No part of this book may be used or reproduced in any manner whatsoever without written permission except in the case of brief quotations embodied in critical articles and reviews. For information, address HarperCollins Publishers, 195 Broadway, New York, NY 10007.

HarperCollins books may be purchased for educational, business, or sales promotional use. For information, please email the Special Markets Department at SPsales@harpercollins.com.

FIRST EDITION

Designed by Nancy Singer

Library of Congress Cataloging-in-Publication Data has been applied for.

ISBN 978-0-06-314011-0

22 23 24 25 26   LSC   10 9 8 7 6 5 4 3 2 1

For Mommy and Gloria, who, had they made it to sixty,
would have been some savvy, sassy sexagenarians

One

The cottages at the Gen pushed up from the earth like new life coming, with their one-floor open-concept designs, and skylights where the ceilings should be, and walls of windows the better to view the trees through. The trees were everything. None of those pale green saplings typical of new housing complexes here. Here the builders set down mature specimens, still fine, though, with voluptuous curvy trunks and jazzy tilts like swagger leans earned by bending, but not breaking, during the storms. The trees gave the development a timeless feel, as if they'd always been here and always would be. And timelessness suited the Gen's target market, who thought themselves like the trees: heirlooms still looking good; still sporting their own curves and swagger; still budding and unfurling and rocking steady supported by massive roots that they hoped would hide their pasts, their secrets. The roots tried, but these people had done some things. And all that wrangling to dig themselves up to move here caused a type of transplant shock. Buried recollections of their younger selves took advantage of the weakened roots and broke away. Repressed images wormed through the mantle of the earth and the years desperate to be seen aboveground, just to be acknowledged for having been.

• • •

Bloc opened the glass doors to the clubhouse and took in the air that smelled like wood from the newly laid Brazilian cherry floors and sweetness from the mimosas floating on silver trays. Today was the monthly lunch reception to welcome the newest residents to the Gen, and the room was loose with laughter and the buzz of twenty separate conversations rising to join the sway of the grand chandelier. Bloc would often turn events like this into a party by showing off his ability at doing the bop and the wobble. And lest someone reduce him to just a Black man who could dance, he also liked to engage in conversation and dazzle the folk with how smart he was. He *was* smart. Considered a genius in the West Philly neighborhood where he'd grown up. Penn Engineering and Sciences, graduate work at MIT, careers at Westinghouse, NASA. But today he wasn't here to dance or prove his intellect. Today he was here to find Tish to make up to her for what happened the other night when he and Tish and Tish's next-door-neighbor Lavia gathered at Tish's cottage the way they'd done on countless evenings. The other night Bloc supplied the weed as usual and they passed the pipe stuffed with healthy buds and watched late-night reruns on TV One and howled at the clownish attire in *Super Fly* as they marveled at the enduring relevance of the Curtis Mayfield soundtrack. They talked politics and philosophy as the wine went down like silk. Tish and Bloc broke down the nuances of Black consciousness for Lavia, who looked South Asian but claimed to be from everywhere and nowhere, as they commenced to solve the world's problems, occasionally spouting motherfucking this and that as if they were forty years younger and living at the high-rise dorm at Penn.

But in the middle of an argument about Hillary versus Bernie, Lavia claimed exhaustion suddenly and left early, left Tish and Bloc alone. Tish switched the music from Pharoah Sanders singing about the creator having a master plan to a not-so-subtle Marvin Gaye begging "let's get it on." She swooned toward Bloc where he sat in the center of her vegan leather couch, pausing to unpin her Sisterlocks that fell around her shoulders like Rapunzel's hair.

His moment had finally come. He'd prepared for the moment every time he'd visit Tish by packing a condom—he knew, after all, that their age group had the highest incidence of sexually transmitted diseases. And he was looking forward to being with a woman his own age again. Thought women his own age deep and knowing with a complexity that he found titillating, especially since his third wife had been twenty years younger and had shredded him. Still shredding him that night as Marvin Gaye sang the part about letting your love come out, and images of Bloc's ex-wife became an out-of-control slideshow clicking through his mind, flattening him so much that even

3

his time-released ED pill that had never let him down . . . let him down.

Tish had been patient, encouraging, asked him if he had some other woman he'd been keeping hid. Well, then, was he impotent? Celibate? Gay? He said no, no, hell no. He just didn't want to ruin the beautiful friendship they had going. She told him she could have handled the other three, but that just-being-friends remark was an insult so he could let himself out.

Today he planned to make it up to Tish. He'd gone to see a holistic practitioner recommended to him by his young boy—his former intern at NASA who was now in his forties and who still repaid Bloc for advancing his career years ago by supplying him with good medical weed. The practitioner prescribed a concoction that Bloc had just started taking.

He felt good right now as he gave a thumbs-up to the organist for his rendition of "Hello Young Lovers." It wasn't the Temptations version that Bloc would listen to as a teen on the 45 player he'd built himself, but it was good enough as he hummed the line that cautions not to cry because he's all alone, because he, too, has had loves of his own. Which he had. He'd married three times trying to find a woman who could replicate his mother's smile. None could, though he'd gotten a princess of a daughter from wife number one, perfection in a son from wife number two, and financial calamity from wife number three because that one had a shopping addiction. She was the only one of the three wives who'd attached herself to his heart.

He shook the thought of her now as he scanned the clubroom, looked past the gaggles sloshing their mimosas around in flutes as they munched on delicate mysteries stuffed in pastry puffs and talked about the midterms, or the conservative shitheads in this part of the state, or the price of *Hamilton* tickets. Then he saw Tish, tall and golden, in the center of the room, the crystal dangles of the chandelier twirling as if they were moved by her too. She was with Lavia, and a new woman Bloc had not yet met. He felt a surge of confidence right now. Had some good weed in his pocket, had his new alabaster pipe, had his condoms, had the medicine he'd started taking coursing through him, had his voice fixed to sing in Tish's ear his own version of "Let's Get It On."

And then he felt it. Couldn't believe what he was feeling. It was as if the confidence he'd just sensed as an unfurling moving up from his toes had gone rogue, gone from an unfurling to a surge. The surge intensified, transitioning as it did to pulsing, from pulsing to throbbing. The throbbing quickened, hardened. Already at his knees, his thighs. *What the hell?*, he thought as it bulged on up to his manhood and held there. His manhood jutting now, without provocation. *What the ever loving hell?*

He restrained himself from looking down to see if it was showing. It couldn't be showing. Hadn't shown since his junior prom when in his tight tuxedo he'd danced slow with Marva, the school's fast girl, and she'd moved against him to the beat of Stevie Wonder singing "My Cherie Amour." Today he was wearing his roomy cargo pants. They could hide a torpedo, but could they hide this? he wondered as he thought that the compounding pharmacist had erred, missed a decimal point or an ingredient. Although he'd been assured its primary ingredient

5

was concentrated citrulline extracted from watermelon. The irony of the recalibrated stereotypes was not lost on him, that a white man had prescribed him watermelon for impotence. Bloc turned to leave. He couldn't approach Tish in such a tumescent state; he'd be her laughingstock, considering the extremes from the nothingness of the other night to the overmuchness of now.

He shielded himself from Tish's view by walking in lock-step with a tall, hefty server, Pedro, according to his name tag. He made small talk with Pedro to calm himself, stopping when Pedro stopped to offer miniature triangles of quiche stuffed with lobster, walking so closely to him that Pedro stopped and said, "Sir, forgive me, but you're crowding me; all I have to offer you is what's on this tray."

"Hey sure," Bloc said, realizing that Pedro thought Bloc was trying to hit on him. "It's not like that, I promise you, believe me, please. Just trying to avoid an asshole," he said, the only thing he could think of to explain the way he'd attached himself to him.

"Welcome to my world," Pedro said, as he turned to answer a woman inquiring if there was anything without shellfish, she was allergic. "There's tons of chicken tempura and the like, sirloin tips wrapped in mushroom, something vegan perhaps? I'll get for you," Pedro called behind him as he sped away, leaving Bloc exposed, but at least he'd almost made it to the glass doors, had the magnificent transplanted Kousa dogwoods in his sight, their white blooms hugging the leaves like corsages pinned to prom gowns; they would hide him if he could just make it to the threshold. He passed the groupings of people laughing in time to the organist playing "I'm Coming Out." He thought the organist must have climbed inside his head with his musical selection. He walked right into Lavia.

He blinked hard as if he could blink Lavia away. He couldn't, as he watched her mouth move. She had a pretty mouth. Her breath smelled of strawberry mimosa and crab salad as she blew into his face asking him what was wrong with him, why was he ignoring her, didn't he hear her calling him. "Tish is over there. Are you coming or what?"

He thought that she put emphasis on *coming* and for a second he wondered if she knew his current torture and was being a smart-ass. She could be a bona fide smart-ass, was always saying something that when unpacked from her proper delivery with her sweet tonal quality and British-tinged accent was surprisingly hilarious. And she did know things; she'd graduated summa cum from Brown.

"I'm leaving," he said.

"No, come, come, come," she insisted. "You must turn this drab affair into a party with your fancy footwork."

"Who am I, Sam and Dave?"

"Sam and Dave? I'm not getting the reference," she said.

"They did a song called 'Soul Man,' okay, I'm not trying to be soul man right now."

"Touchy, touchy," she said, as she pulled his arm. "Dance or not, I don't care. But I do want you to meet our new resident, Cynthia; she's a true delight. Grew up in Western Philadelphia. Didn't you grow up in Western Philadelphia?"

"West Philadelphia, Lavia, not Western, West. There's no such place called Western Philadelphia."

"Ooh, listen to you, you are the moody one today."

He told her he didn't feel well, as he tried not to concentrate on the throbbing coming from what now might as well be a third leg.

"What is it? You don't have a squeezing sensation in your chest, do you, because you're perspiring all of a sudden and the air is on full blast in here." Lavia stopped where she was and motioned for Tish.

He tried to ask Lavia not to involve Tish, but before he could form the words, Tish and the new woman, Cynthia, were next to Lavia in a loose circle around Bloc. "He says he's leaving, claims to be ill," Lavia said.

"Ill? What the hell is wrong with you, Bloc?" Tish asked. "You need to go to the top of the O."

"Top of the O?" Cynthia asked, and Bloc could feel her eyes drop to where his cargo pants jutted.

"Yeah," Tish said. "You know how the development is arranged in the shape of the numeral sixty, which I find too cutesy for my tastes, but in any event, the doc's office sits at the top of the O."

"Right," Cynthia said. "I'd forgotten there's a whole new concept in addresses here, because I live at the bottom of the stem." She extended her hand. "I'm Cynthia. Nice to meet you. Lavia tells me you're also from West Philly."

Cynthia laughed when she said it and Bloc almost wanted to ask her what was so funny even as he took in her wide smile and her wide halo of a 'fro and her wide hips shaped like half-moons. He stopped himself from appraising her wideness, shook

8

her hand, told her his name, and watched her tame her mouth back to a simple smile. He was about to apologize for having to leave so abruptly before they even sat down to eat when he heard Lavia gasp.

"Oh my, Bloc," Lavia said, her voice shaking as she laughed. "You appear to be stuck in the up?"

"Stuck in the up?" Cynthia asked then. Asked it quickly, too quickly, Bloc thought. "Is that an address, too? Where would that be?"

"It's not an address, it's an illusion," Tish said. "Trust me, I've been to that house, knocked on that door, ain't nobody home."

"Goodness, you're too cold, Tish," Lavia said.

"Actually, I'm too hot, I'm going for a swim," Tish said, as she turned to leave, flinging her hand in the air as she did. She was wearing a black-and-white tiger print dress that looked to Bloc like an open-mouthed laugh, mocking him even as she walked away, her long back moving from side to side in exaggerated swipes. He felt as if the throbbing in his manhood was making its way up, pausing in the pit of his stomach. He imagined that soon enough the squeezing sensation really would be in the center of his chest. Good. He'd always hoped for a quick, sudden death. No lingering for him the way his mother had lingered, stuck in the tunnel for weeks making that heartbreaking sound of the death rattle. He'd already planned that should he get such a devastating prognosis, he'd settle his affairs, spend time with his son and daughter, then rent an RV and drive cross-country to the Grand Canyon where he'd take his final flight into the center of that majestic hole. He felt his eyes water as he listened to Lavia say that she was going to have a seat, they were about to start serving. The air was leaving the clubroom. He was dying, Bloc was sure, and he wanted to speak to his children, thank them for loving him despite his inability to stay married to their mothers. He wanted to see his third wife, just one more time, even after she'd crushed him.

Her name was Coral, and she had a shopping addiction that was so severe that when she couldn't get to Nordstrom, she craved sex, but not with Bloc. She'd cruise, of all places, churches, for her release. Bloc had followed her one Sunday morning. He was seeing her now, sprawled on the back seat of the 7 Series BMW he'd given her for her fortieth birthday.

He started sobbing. Couldn't believe that he was standing in the Sexagenarian's clubroom sobbing like an eight-year-old. The croaking sounds pushing through his lips were so loud he could barely hear Cynthia talking to him.

She was asking him had it been more than four hours. Her voice was soft and whispery. Comforting.

"No," he said, though he garbled even that monosyllable.

"I just know, you know, that the advertisers caution to seek medical attention if, you know, the results last longer than four hours."

"It's not that, you know, it's not Viagra." His breath caught in his throat and he felt as if he was choking.

"I didn't mean to presume. But, regardless, maybe some fresh air would help," she said, as she offered him a tissue.

"There's no such thing as fresh air anymore; the delicate balance of atmospheric gases has been irrecoverably skewed." He wiped his face. He wasn't dying as he felt the pressure in his chest ease, his breaths settle into a more rhythmic in and out. Cynthia was looking at him. She had the darkest eyes he'd ever seen on a brown-skinned woman. They were stark, hard, balanced out by her softly formed mouth; her lips curved in a smile that pushed her sadness to the corners of her mouth. They all had their sadness after all. Sometimes the sadness hid out as it did in the creases around Cynthia's smile, or in the jerky sound of Lavia's laughter, or the heat of Tish's sighs. Other times it was as pronounced as his ill-timed erection, humiliating, throbbing.

"I'm sorry," he said then. "I didn't mean to snap at you. Perhaps some outside air would actually help. You'll join me?"

Cynthia lowered her head, indicating neither acquiescence nor rejection, and they stepped outside where a soft drizzle was playing mind games with the sun.

Two

Cynthia hadn't intended to invite Bloc in after he walked her home. But she'd envied his ability to cry. She'd wanted to cry, too, as it sank in during the reception that she'd actually moved here. Egged on by her son, E, she'd let go of her gorgeous mansion-sized three-story West Philly twin where she'd lived for thirty years, five of those happily after her divorce. She'd traded her vibrant block, filled with the eclectic street sounds of double Dutch chants from the little girls, and the high-volume Black music from the white Penn students, and the linguistic smorgasbord coming from the Lutheran church on the corner that served as a sanctuary for undocumented immigrants, for this pristine development with its terrifying newness. So she invited Bloc in because she'd cried vicariously through him as he sobbed all over his orange-and-cream-colored gingham shirt. And she'd always had an affinity for gingham, its thoughtful predictability, the conscientious innocence of its pattern.

She focused on the kindness of those tiny squares as she ushered Bloc to her center-island counter and apologized for the condition of her unpacked cottage with the boxes still taped shut and the furniture still shrink-wrapped. He insisted no apology was necessary and then he offered her weed.

She thought that she should be more shocked that she accepted even though she knew very little about him. Knew only that he'd lived here for two years, was friends with Lavia, and had a maybe/maybe not relationship with Tish, whom Cynthia had zeroed in on when she stepped into the reception and moved her head methodically from side to side the way the Secret Service would. Though Cynthia wasn't looking for assassins, just another Black person. "Please God, can there be even just one, for goodness' sake," she'd whined under her breath, a throwback prayer from college and early years in her career. She saw the upsweep of Tish's Sisterlocks then. She thought the hair Tish's attempt to make sure that she wasn't mistaken for white, and Cynthia respected the effort. Shortly she met Lavia, and then Bloc. And here she sat an hour later perplexed that she was not shocked that she'd agreed to get high with him even though she hadn't smoked weed in more than forty years. Forty! The passage of time, though, was shocking.

She watched him deftly stuff healthy marijuana buds into a pipe that looked as expensive as her tourmaline center-island counter. The counter was a builder's upgrade that E had talked her into though she would have been fine with Formica, finer still with the worn butcher-block counter in the house where she wanted to be right now.

Bloc swiveled the counter stool to face her. "Okay, first you take the pipe," he said, jokingly.

"It's been a minute, but I think I remember needing the

pipe in my hand as a requisite first step," she said, as she hurriedly inched the pipe toward her mouth. But her hands were sweaty, the pipe was slick; she fumbled the pipe and dropped it and closed her ears to the sound of it crashing against the floor. Except that Bloc caught it before it hit the floor, almost spilled off the counter stool himself, and Cynthia looked away lest her eyes fall to his pants where she'd refused to look since Tish humiliated him at the reception.

"No harm, no foul," he said, before she could apologize. "May I?" he asked, as he leaned in and offered the pipe.

Cynthia nodded and Bloc gently pulled her chin to separate her lips so that he could ease the pipe between them. His thumb press was like fire against her chin, rerouting neural connections, and she felt the warmth of it deep in her chest. She had not an inkling what to do with the feeling, so she focused on the gingham shirt and pulled hard on the pipe, then felt the smoke rise to her head and through her head. She thought if she looked up she'd see the curly ends of her 'fro rising toward the skylights.

"Mmm, good, you're doing it like a pro," Bloc whispered. He eased the pipe from between her lips and she already missed his thumb. "How you doing? You good?" he asked, as he blew out a mouthful of smoke and handed the pipe back to Cynthia.

"Ah, my goodness, are you kidding me. I'm better than good, that's some potent stuff." She had forgotten the feel of a good weed high, the slackened facial muscles that defaulted to a dopey smile, the sudden hunger, the inhibitions unclothed. She'd partaken regularly back in undergraduate school after spending the day stroking to keep from drowning in sea after sea of white privilege and attitude; she'd return to her campus apartment where one of her roommates browned cheese toast in a buttered skillet and the other's boyfriend rolled stogies from the half-ounce bag they'd all put in to buy with change they'd pinched from their work/study paychecks. She'd toke then, suddenly aware how depleting all that inequality was.

Cynthia took in Bloc's presence as she unfurled a mouthful of smoke. His lips were surprisingly thin; everything else about him, his forehead, his cheeks, his nose, had a beefy thickness to them. His eyes were a lighter brown than they should be given his solid brown complexion; his gray-and-white mustache had been trimmed expertly over his thin lips, his lips pursed as he blew out smoke, directing it skylight-ward. She shook off the urge to ask for the feel of his thumb against her chin as she gave him a deep smile instead, actually smiling more at the shirt than at him. The gingham smiled back as his chest rose and fell with his breaths. Bloc returned her smile with a wink but she didn't catch it because she was too preoccupied with her tongue and the way it seemed fused to the roof of her mouth, making her realize how thirsty she was. "Damn, let me get us water," she said, as she retrieved two small bottles from the under-counter refrigerator. She apologized that she hadn't unpacked glasses just yet.

"Glasses are overrated," Bloc said through an uncontainable smile. "I've drank from many a bottle in my day, more often than not those bottles were covered in brown paper bags."

"Really?" Cynthia said, her lips smirked to one side. "I wouldn't have figured you for the corner boy type."

"Well, vivacious beauty that you are, one wouldn't have figured you for a quiet girl, but I'm willing to bet you were."

Cynthia laughed an extended laugh and pushed back from the counter. "I better find us something to eat before you talk yourself into trouble." She opened and closed cabinets that she already knew to be empty as she swatted away the regret that she always felt if she sensed a man found her attractive. Even now in her weed-induced state of confused euphoria she felt it. Deep down she believed she was an ugly girl, just pretending to have a pleasing look, and soon enough whoever seemed enamored by her, the way Bloc did, would discover that her beauty—he had just called her a beauty—was a sham. She thought her face a jumble of contraries the way the softly formed mouth and full, jutting lips mixed it up with the sharp nose and overly defined cheekbones and severely dark eyes. Her complexion didn't help. It was so middle of the road that it served no good purpose; she'd always wished it had taken a stand firmly on one side of the road or the other and been either blue black or butter. Her hair, though, had taken a stand. It was thick and wild and barely held a hot press before Afros were even a style. As a child she was accustomed to people smiling at her before the standard what-a-cute-little-girl remark and then stopping before they said it because it took a minute for her looks to register and for them to decide that she wasn't, after all, cute.

Her looks had been as burdensome as the mother she had. She was teased for her looks growing up, for her evil-looking eyes and untamed hair. She was teased for her mother, too, because her mother, Divine, was bipolar; she kept a dark house and changed men like stockings. Cynthia hadn't learned that her mother's behavior had a name until she was practically an adult. She thought that the clinical diagnosis excused her mother some. There was no clinical term for ugly, though.

"Okay, like I said, I just got here yesterday, so I don't gots lots," she said, turning to face Bloc, embarrassed still that he'd called her a beauty.

"We could walk over to the shops," Bloc offered. "They've got a decent bakery, a smoothie stand, a candy store that replicates the ones from back in the day when you could get a nickel candy bar, though I guarantee you a PayDay candy bar over there will cost five bucks."

"Oh my god, I loved PayDays; I would pick the nuts off that caramel log, and then go to heaven on that log."

"My favorite was Good & Plenty, damn, that licorice was serious," he said on a laugh.

Cynthia was about to agree to them walking over to the shops, but the drizzle that had started up when they'd left the reception had transitioned into a steady rain and now made crackling sounds against the skylights. Then she remembered the zucchini bread she'd bought at a roadside stand the day before when her son drove her here. The look of it had reminded her of her grandmother's bread pudding, though her son had cautioned that there was no quality control. "Just a loaf wrapped in cellophane, Mom, really? It doesn't even list the contents; you have no way of knowing what's in it."

She told Bloc the story as she fumbled with the wrapping covering the loaf, explaining that they ordinarily wouldn't have stopped but she was shaken when the car struck and killed the cutest woodchuck.

"Woodchuck? That's a shame," Bloc said as he came and stood next to her.

"I know; it landed on the hood of the car and I was staring into its eyes, the softest brown eyes. And its little ears were quivering so I made my son sit there and let it finish dying before he cleaned it off the car. And then its ears stood straight up as if they'd heard something of interest."

"Gabriel's trumpet for woodchucks, perhaps?"

"I think that was it exactly," Cynthia said. "And I realized, damn, my ears are gonna stand straight up like that one day."

"Who knew, right?"

"Oh my god, I said a similar thing to my son as we watched the little creature die, and he was like, well, of course we're all gonna die, Mom."

"But not us, right?" Bloc said, as he leaned in to help Cynthia undo the plastic wrap. "Myself, I've only recently moved beyond the intellectual concept of it all, and you know, and have begun to accept that, damn, this party called life on earth is actually gonna end for me, too." He said it emphatically. "I used to think that the eat, drink, and be merry 'cause tomorrow you die thing was just something irresponsible gluttons trudged out when they wanted to overindulge. But you know what," he said as he laughed, "each day the odds increase that tomorrow I might die."

Cynthia nodded, enjoying the sound of his laughter. He had a gumbo laugh, thick with a mixture of tones and pauses that felt honest the way it stopped on the right beat, neither extending beyond its usefulness, nor ending too soon. Now they both focused in on the sight of the finally unwrapped zucchini loaf as if it were some idolatrous object they were about to pray to. "Damn," Bloc whispered, "should we go for it or what?"

"I mean, I really want to, but I'll be dammed, I haven't unpacked a single fork," Cynthia said.

"You got fingers? A fork is redundant right now," Bloc said, as he tore off a chunk and dropped it in his mouth. "Mmm, that's some good stuff."

Cynthia followed suit. "Oh my god, is it ever." Their arms stroked against each other's as they alternated pulling at the loaf and Cynthia mused about her son's unwillingness to buy it just because it didn't list the ingredients. "But he's a patent attorney. I guess the loaf didn't come with a contact, I mean contract," she said, as they both howled at her mistake.

They talked about their children then. Bloc confessing regret that he'd not been more involved in the growing-up years. Cynthia remarking that her ex-husband had been the opposite; he'd been so involved, so excessively protective, that she feared it had made her son too uptight, unwilling to take risks.

"But you kicked your husband to the curb, right?" Bloc said on a laugh. "And I can say that, 'cause I been kicked to the curb twice, by good women too. Not undeservedly, either."

"Yeah? Were you one of those wanting a do-right woman, as Aretha sings, when you not a do-right man?"

"Damn, lady, how you got me pegged so right? That was me, except for my third wife. I did more than right by her," Bloc said, as he told Cynthia about the house he'd built for her on Cherry

Tree Lane. Cynthia noticed sadness welling up in his eyes as he talked so she told him about her West Philadelphia mansion that her ex-husband had picked out and that he must have really, really loved her back then because he'd always dreamed of living someplace where the streets were named Cherry Tree Lane, but instead agreed to settle right in West Philly.

They were down to the crumbs of the zucchini loaf and Cynthia scooped them up and tried to share them with Bloc but she dropped them midway to his mouth and she watched them fall and cling to his pristine orange-and-cream-colored shirt. She hastened to dust the crumbs away. She looked down as she did, down, down, and down where she'd not allowed herself to look since she'd witnessed his emotional breach during the reception. It was still there, one protruding mass. "Aw," she said then. "Is it uncomfortable?"

He made a deep sound from the back of his throat that was half cough, half moan as he sucked in his breath and said, "Like nobody's business," and she could see his heartbeat quicken as the checks on his shirt went into a flutter.

"Can I do anything to help?" she asked, as she inched in closer.

"Uh, uh, Jesus. You know, it's like they say, don't start nothing, won't be nothing, uh, all I'm saying is that you know, you're in charge here, just so you know, I'm totally down with Me Too, you know, just weed in that pipe, I swear—"

"I know," Cynthia said as she moved her hands through the air, through the years. So many years of being a good girl until that one time when she was not, when she sullied the fullness of her young womanhood with Mr. Z, an older man who had a wife and a kid who'd made her feel beautiful. It had devastated her. She rushed her hands through that thicket of time lest she be trapped there. Then the shame she felt over her mother's behavior rushed to fill the space. Even after she accepted that Divine was not a horrible person, that she was just sick, Cynthia still faulted herself. That tiny part of her that embraced irrationality believed that if she were a better, smarter, cuter, more personable, more inventive, more empathetic daughter, she could have cured her mother herself. She pushed that shame to the side to make way for her hands. But then her time as a wife sprang before her, married to a man with serious political aspirations who faulted her for not being the soft and assertive social butterfly that a man such as him needed. She'd never been sure what he meant by soft and inferred he meant her look, which was unalterable except for her hair. So she suffered through years of burns on her scalp from superstrength permanent relaxers to get her hair bone straight until she'd had enough of the harsh chemicals and instead went to the Dominican hair shops with their high-heat straightening methods that thinned her hair to wisps of its former self, finally settling for a weave but was mortified when she looked at herself in the mirror; she screamed then, *Lord Jesus, help me, I have become a Black woman with a weave*. She knew that when she patiently detached the weave and allowed her own hair to stand in its truth the way it was always meant to, her marriage would end.

She shoved away thoughts of her marriage. But a new thicket sprang in front of her then filled with the years raising her son, who'd done well, except that he tried of late to take over her husband's place after the divorce and direct her moves, convincing her to move away from her house that was her solace and her joy to this place with its veneered sterility. Even texting her this morning in all caps to go to the reception and make new friends as if she were headed to the first day of kindergarten. She wondered what E would say about her making a new friend out of this man standing in front of her in all his bulging glory. She plied that air back that was heavy, glad that she'd bought the zucchini cake.

She was standing so close to Bloc that the checks on his shirt seemed to run together and blend like an orange soda poured over a double scoop of butter pecan ice cream, her favorite little-girl treat. She imagined herself sitting on the cracked red leather stool at the five-and-dime slurping down the ice cream soda, now putting both her hands around the hard cold of the fountain glass. Except that in this moment what she'd just grabbed was very far from a fountain glass, very far from cold. And were these her own hands? she wondered as she wrapped her hands around what she held—and now squeezed. Was this her own voice saying, "Mercy," drawing the word out the way her grandmother would. She noted the irony of invoking her grandmother's memory in such a situation. But what she was about to do might warrant a little mercy as the crumbs resting against the checkered pattern of the gingham shirt took on the shape of a winking eye.

They were a tangle then as their arms wrapped, their mouths missed, missed, then connected. He ran his hands through her woolly hair. She undid the buttons on his shirt, then she looked around and said, "Damn, there's no place to lay."

"The floor," he said, out of breath.

"Negro, please, you must think I'm nineteen; I need some cushioning under my back."

"Don't you have a bed?"

"It's in the bedroom."

"Lead the way." He pulled her by the hand.

"No, it's not put together."

"You mean the movers didn't—"

"I didn't let them—"

"You didn't let—"

"No, it would make the move here too real."

"Okay, well, invite me into your state of un-realness, Miss Lady, and just tell me where you been sleeping?"

"That chair." Cynthia pointed to the only piece of furniture that was sans shrink wrap in the great room, a retro orange corduroy swivel chair with matching ottoman. They both stared at the chair, heads tilted, as if deciding on its suitability was akin to figuring out the meaning of life.

"Ooh, ooh, wait," she said, eyes popping, mouth agape, "I have an air mattress."

"Sounds like a plan; is it still packed?"

"Hell if I remember."

They laughed as she pointed to a corner where the air mattress was boxed. Her son had bought it for her in the event she had sleepover guests. More laughter after Bloc hit the lever and the mattress rose and rose. They jumped in the center of the mattress as if they were outside playing in one of the pools.

The laughter stilled then and the room went silent save the

rustling sounds of clothes being shed, and the thump and sizzle of the rain hitting the skylights. They managed to hold at bay the awkward air hanging over them, that they were essentially strangers. They wrapped themselves instead in the primal familiarity of lips stroking, hands clutching, hips rocking—carefully because Bloc's hip was relatively new, and Cynthia's back was prone to go out. Plus, she was about to panic that she wouldn't be able to accommodate Bloc as engorged as he seemed. Was about to push him away and say that it was all a bad idea, she didn't want to be torn apart. But his mouth and his hands, even his breath, had found all the parts of her that cried out to be kissed and stroked and held on to. She held on then. And the summit held too. And there she was in the center of a borealis, or was it in the center of her, as she gasped and called out for Jesus.

· · ·

Cynthia giggled to herself in her half-high, half-not state, enjoying the feel of the tingles receding from the surface of her skin. She watched the sky showing off through the skylights. It was orange with trembles of red as the rain had passed over. She listened to the sounds coming from one of the pools, giggles and yelps as if the people who lived here had reverted to lives of youthful indulgences. She snickered that she'd become one of them. She couldn't wait to text Gabriella. Gabriella was her best friend from childhood on who now lived in Santa Fe to be closer to her daughter and triplet grandchildren. Cynthia smiled and said, damn, as she started composing the text in her head. She turned over and snuggled closer to Bloc on the air mattress. She laid her head on Bloc's shoulder. He was completely still, and she realized that he hadn't moved since he'd rolled over.

"Hey," she whispered, her voice low and urgent, as she gently pushed at his head. "You still alive?" She laughed when she said it, praying that it was a joke. "Hello," she said, louder now, as she yanked him and his head fell against her chest, and she was about to scream out his name, but now she felt Bloc's lips brush her chest; they were warm, moist with trickles of spit, and now he moved his head and she felt her own breaths loosen in relief.

"Hi there," she whispered.

"Mmm." His voice was muffled as he nestled his head against her. His hair was surprisingly soft and tickled her neck. "I have this thing where I pass out after."

"Pass out? As in completely unconscious?"

"Yeah, hasn't happened in years, but then again it hasn't been this good in years."

Cynthia smirked. "Years? Really? I like flattery, but years? Must be the Viagra, or Cialis, or whatever you'd taken that backfired. Bet you'll leave that stuff alone."

"No, pretty lady, it was all you. I swear to you." He lifted his head. "Are these lying eyes?"

"No, they're 'telltale you been smoking weed Visine-needing' red eyes," she said, as she eased off the air mattress. "I've got some here somewhere." She went to the bathroom and then started pouring herself back into her clothes, the stretchy denim pencil skirt, the paisley peasant top that fell loosely over the skirt and hid the protrusion at the bottom of her stomach. She bypassed the shapewear for now, wanting to cover herself quickly thinking that might encourage him to get up and dressed and leave. She wanted to take a shower, unpack another box of things, at least call the concierge and have them send someone over to put her bed together. She stepped into her sandals and rummaged through the box marked bathroom cabinet. The sun had returned as if to retrieve a forgotten fedora and warmed her face as it pounced through the wall-to-wall, floor-to-ceiling window.

"Ah, here it is," she said, as she pulled the Visine from the box. She turned toward the air mattress. He was on his back, snoring. "Jeez," she said under her breath. She didn't consider herself prudish, but his excessive full-frontal, beefy exhibition was disconcerting and made her turn away. She'd have to wake him or cover him. Plus, his stereophonic snoring was so loud now that she couldn't hear anything outside of this room: not the people at the pool, not the birds flocking to the birdbath out back, not the sing, sing of the wind chimes, not even the car door closing on the other side of the hedges that flanked her carriage house. Nor did she hear the *beep, beep* of the car remote, the footsteps approaching the patio just on the other side of this windowed wall. Her peripheral vision, though, compensated at that moment for what she did not hear as she saw motion on her patio, familiar motion, tall, exacting, logical, careful motion. Motion spawned from her that was her opposite. Her son, E, walking across her patio.

"Holy shit," she said in a loud whisper, as she ran to the air mattress and swatted Bloc's shoulder. "You've got to get up, now, my son's here. You gotta get the hell out." He smiled in his sleep and shifted, opening his legs even wider as if he were doing a modified version of the yoga happy baby pose.

E was tapping on the door, saying, "Mom, it's me." Cynthia would have to pretend she wasn't home. But now she heard the lock disengage, remembered that they'd added his image to the face-recognition technology. She watched the doorknob turn, thinking how stupid she was to have credentialed him, how much she hated this place, and could she make it to the chair to retrieve the quilt she'd slept under to at least throw over Bloc's expansive nakedness. But she wouldn't be able to get to it in time. The door was opening. "Mom?"

Cynthia threw herself out the door the way she would have thrown herself in front of a truck to protect E from getting hit. He fell backward toward the hedges and Cynthia grabbed him, hugged him. "Oh my darling son, how did you know that I needed you here at this moment to take me to CVS?"

"CVS? Huh?"

"Yes, I need some stuff that they want an arm and a leg for here at the apothecary. Probably just call it an apothecary so that they can triple the price of everything."

"I'll pay," E said, looking at his mother as if she were a curiosity. "CVS is at least ten miles—"

"Oh, so you corralled me into moving here, and now you can't drive me ten miles?"

"Mom, I did not—"

"Where's your car?"

"It's there, right in your driveway; wait, are you all right? I've been calling you forever. And why are your eyes so red?"

"I forgot to unmute my phone after that welcoming reception thing that you insisted I attend. And as for my eyes, if you must know, I've been crying," Cynthia said, as she walked ahead of him.

"Mom, crying? Why?" he asked, as he hit the remote and Cynthia jumped in the car. E was just a second behind her.

"Because this is hard for me. I've left a life. Do you understand that?" The sound of the seat belt clicking punctuated her words as Cynthia crossed her arms in front of her chest to hide that she was braless and adjusted the air vent toward her hoping that she didn't smell of marijuana or worse.

They were both quiet as E pulled away from her cottage and drove around the elevated curve that allowed 360 views of the stunning topography. The sales office and decorated cottage sat at the high point and Cynthia resisted giving the middle finger to the sample home that had wooed her with its sun-kissed colors and windowed walls and skylights that allowed for stargazing.

She was remembering when she and E first toured the place. She'd mumbled yeah, yeah, yeah to his gushing over the smart house technology complete with a talking fridge capable of placing an order for milk and eggs; the walk-in tub that could draw a bath on voice command; the Sleep-Matic beds dressed like queens; the option to upgrade the flooring to rare chestnut that had been reclaimed from Abraham Lincoln's log cabin home. The floors weren't really Lincoln's, but Cynthia thought they may as well have been the way E and the sales associate were gawking over them. She'd drifted away from their incessant oohing and turned down a dimly lit hallway that led to the laundry room shadowed in blue light and reminded her of the blue-light basement house parties of her youth. The smells did, too, apple incense with a punch of the burnt rope scent of marijuana. The walls were painted mauve and matched the washer and dryer, and all looked purple under the blue light. She'd realized then that the laundry room was every bit as staged as the rest of the cottage where digital frames flashed photos of adorable racially ambiguous children tagged world's greatest grandkids. NPR drizzled through the rest of the model, but back there Nina Simone's "You'd Be So Nice to Come Home To" crackled through the speaker, looping continuously to the line that wailed, *you'd be paradise.*

She'd groaned under her breath at the heavy-handed staging and smirked at the framed posters leaning against the washing machine, certain that the posters had been placed exactly there because some millennial marketing professional predicted that people like her would rifle through them. She couldn't wait to text Gabriella about the overkill. She especially missed Gabriella at such times and could almost hear Gabriella saying, *Fuck it, let's see what the dumbass posters say.* Cynthia laughed out loud at the thought as she rifled through a psychedelic print spelling out FREE YOUR MIND, a raised fist emblazoned with POWER TO THE PEOPLE—a curious selection she thought since from what she could see, nothing but white people were looking to buy here. She lingered over the next one, a red-and-black peace sign urging MAKE LOVE NOT WAR. She was suddenly transported to her grandmother's block where she'd escape to spend summer afternoons when her mother had been too many days with the blinds drawn. Her grandmother would fix her a helping of bread pudding with lemon sauce and they'd sip iced tea and watch the *Edge of Night* together as Rose teased her to laughter by commenting on the people in the soap opera, calling one a stupid heifer, another a no-good cow, in that thick Geechee accent that Cynthia loved. Soon Cynthia's chest had opened sufficiently for her to return home.

She'd walk past the house on the corner where Macon lived. He was older than her by three years and had survived a bout of polio so that his left foot faced inward and his left arm was perpetually folded against his side. He had wide shoulders and a boxy head and the prettiest lips she'd ever seen on a boy. He'd stand on his porch under the shade of the locust tree and blow into a flute and she thought that his paralyzed arm had been shaped just to hold that flute. He seemed to be a loner, like she was a loner. The other girls except for Gabriella shunned Cynthia because they said her mother was a whore. She guessed Macon had suffered through a similar alienation because of the way his foot dragged, and the permanent bend in his arm. Sometimes she'd pause at the corner and listen to him play.

They'd never speak otherwise from the time she was ten until the summer she turned sixteen. He was a pre-college boy that summer with a big Afro and melon-sized muscles in his good arm that he showed off in the fringed suede vests he wore. She sat on his steps that day as he played "Hey There Lonely Girl." When he finished, he walked down the steps and touched her shoulder. She turned calmly; she'd been expecting this for years. He motioned her toward the house and she followed him right through the living room that smelled of salt pork and buttered grits and up the stairs to his bedroom where the fading Jack and Jill wallpaper shouted with posters proclaiming BLACK IS BEAUTI- FUL, and FREE HUEY, and there it was, MAKE LOVE NOT WAR, that same poster that she was staring at in the laundry room of the decorated model of the Gen with Nina Simone's voice pushing through her head singing, *so nice, you'd be paradise.* She'd curled up on Macon's bed and let him kiss her. His lips were thick and salty like seared steak fat. His hand was both gentle and insistent as he whispered in her ear, his hand pulsing against her then until she came in glitters and she thought she would love him forever.

Her son had walked into the laundry room then.

"There you are, Mom," E said, and Cynthia knew that as he looked at her face under the blue light, he was mistaking her expression as love for the house—he was her son after all and therefore not emotionally equipped to consider that her ex- pression had anything to do with her sexuality. "Finally, Mom," he said, grinning like a ten-year-old. "I think we've found your new home."

She glanced at E now as he turned out of the development. He so looked like his father right now: tall and slim and poised with his polite features and reddened complexion and silky hair. She'd always been grateful that he'd taken his father's looks.

"So how was it?" He broke the silence first.

"How was what?" she said, as she pictured Bloc sprawled open-legged and snoring on her air mattress. She swallowed hard, hoping she hadn't sounded defensive.

"The reception."

"It was a reception. How are receptions generally? A bunch of people standing around making nice talking about the weather or similar superficialities."

"Did you meet people at least?"

"No one of note," she snapped. Then apologized. "I don't mean to be so bitchy. How's Melanie?"

"She's well; in fact she asked me to let you know that whenever you're available she'll take you to get your hair done."

"I do not want her to take me to get my hair done," Cynthia said, as she patted at her hair and tried to smooth it down. She'd forgotten that beyond the red eyes, beyond being out without a bra or even panties, her hair must be wilder than usual especially since Bloc had run his hands all through her hair. *Lady, I love your Angela Davis hair*, he'd said.

"Well, Melanie said something about them not having a Black stylist here, apparently she checked—"

"She would—"

"Only because she said you've insisted that only a Black person can do your hair—"

"Only a Black person can—"

"Well, the place Melanie goes—"

"Melanie and I have different hair, E. Okay."

"I know, but yours can be so nice when it's, you know, straightened out."

"It's a 'fro, E."

"I know but it's so, you know, nappy."

"That's the point of a 'fro, to be nappy. Tell Melanie to take her own mother to get her hair done."

Cynthia turned away to look out the window. Cornfields rose taller and denser like weaponized versions of themselves and Cynthia felt locked in and vulnerable. Her breaths came faster and she hoped she wasn't descending into some weed-induced paranoia.

"So what brought you all the way here so soon after dropping me off?" she asked, as she tried to gird her voice with cheeriness, trying also to ignore the corn spears and now the vultures circling suddenly, as if they anticipated a death was soon to come, or they knew of one that had already happened and they were just getting here, after decades, to pick at the waiting corpse.

"Well, I just got news, and since you weren't answering your phone I figured I'd come and tell you in person that there's an offer on the house."

"My house?" Cynthia couldn't keep the desperation from her voice.

"Of course, your house."

"So soon, we just listed it."

"Mom, this is a good thing, they're willing to meet the asking price, and even waive inspections because they'd like a quick settlement, which would be helpful because I don't have to tell you about the astronomical homeowners association fees here—"

"Oh, now the fees are an issue; they weren't an issue when you were pushing me to buy the damn place—" She stopped talking. She was about to cry. She couldn't let E see her cry. She knew all too well how heart-shattering it was to watch your own mother cry. "You know what, take me back," she blurted.

"Back where?"

"To the Sexagenarian place where you forced me to move—"

"Mom—"

"Please, E, just take me back, before I put you out of this car and drive myself back to Philly and see how you feel stranded in such a place as this."

"Mom, you're being really unfair here," he said as he made a U-turn. "I mean, you agreed to everything."

They were silent as they headed toward the setting sun that was making an orange and yellow mess as it splattered itself against the back of the sky. Cynthia thought of her own heart up there, dripping, staining, until the night would rush in and mop it all away. Right now she missed her house like she would miss a beloved relative who'd just died, desperate for the things she'd never expected to miss: the howling sounds coming from her next-door neighbor's house, where a daughter had returned with an infant who was being sleep trained and wailed all night long; she wanted more than anything this moment to hear that baby cry. She missed the smell of butter toffee that her neighbor cooked up weekly to package in colorful tins and sell at the farmers' market to defray the exploding real estate taxes. She missed the way her house soothed her after long days of throwing elbows at the nonprofit she'd directed, where she'd have to constantly overexplain to her white colleagues the merits of a grant application submitted by Black groups. She'd grow infuriated because they were well-meaning, supposedly progressive people, but they were incapable of understanding the world outside of their privilege. Her house would welcome her home like it was a person with a thumping heart, and misty warm breath, and wide-open give-me-a-hug arms.

34

Cynthia couldn't hold back the tears. She pretended to sneeze to have an excuse to reach for the tissue box on the console. As she blew her nose and wiped her eyes she conceded that her house had also let her down the way anything that a person loves too much will let them down. But she'd adored that center staircase that was double-wide and smelled of pine in the early morning and echoed the sounds of her footsteps that were like low notes on a xylophone. *Don't love things, love Jesus*, her grandmother used to say. And Cynthia had had that actual thought when at the height of her affection for those stairs, they'd thrown her like she was a rag doll, landing her at the Gen.

She'd been running up the stairs from the first floor to the third right up the center because she enjoyed the press of her feet against the steps where they dipped the slightest bit; she thought the center of the steps held her history in the house. Plus she could feel the grandeur of the staircase from the center. But right when she was three steps from the top the house tilted, which is how she experienced bouts of benign paroxysmal positional vertigo. *Small crystals in the inner ear loosen and make your head spin, but as the name suggests, completely benign*, they'd told her at the ER where E and Melanie insisted she go when it first happened the year before.

But there was nothing benign about a dizzy spell three steps from the top on a double-wide staircase. She had reached for the banister, the stunning hand-turned banister that she and Ethrow had restored with so much love when they'd first bought the house. The banister pulled away, just as Ethrow had twenty years into their marriage, and became impossible to reach. So she reached for a miracle. She pulled back air. The air was lightweight and useless and horribly noisy, filled with a *boom, boom, booming* that she realized was the sound of a body in quick descent, in a hurry it seemed to meet the rapturous darkness as her head crashed into the wall at the bottom of the stairwell where the sun looked on.

The concussion had not been the worst of the fall, even though Cynthia couldn't tolerate bright lights or loud noises or thinking deeply for weeks after. The unrelenting pain of the cracked ribs was not the worst, nor the chorus of bruises, each trying to outsing the other, all off-key, screeching unbearably. As consequential as the ruptured spleen had been—it came closest to killing her—it was not the worst.

The worst was that E gained the edge in their ongoing discussion-dispute about the house being too large. Before the fall, it had been too easy to swat away his lawyerly, logical appeal: sixtysomething-year-old with vertigo living alone in a three-story mansion-sized house with its outsized carbon footprint not to mention the return on investment she was forgoing because the house was so close to Penn. Did she know that if she put in a new kitchen she could get seven figures for the house? But after her fall he went straight for the heart. Retold the terror of finding her crumpled on the landing, eyes wide open, purple splashes already formed under the skin on her face, and at first he thought he'd lost her. Could she even imagine what that was like? She could. She'd found her own mother time and again from a different kind of falling. She didn't want E to spend the prime of his life when his marriage was young and his dreams had a lot of unfolding yet to do worrying about his mother living alone in an oversized house suffering from a condition that made her prone to dizzy spells.

E was back at the high curve of the development with its breathtaking landscape made more spectacular by the transplanted trees. He cleared his throat. "Mom, I'm sorry you're not happy here." His voice cracked then and Cynthia turned to look at him. He smiled the way he would when he was her adorable little boy, when he really wanted to cry but held it in so as not to make her sad. The gesture melted her. She realized this was hard for him, too, having to accept that his mother was no longer thirty-five, that she was in fact growing old. "I just think you should give it some time," he continued. "Remember when I was twelve and went for the first time to sleepover camp and wanted to come home after the first night, but you made me stay because you said I had to give it seventy-two hours, and then on, like, the seventy-first hour it suddenly got good?"

"I do remember," she said. And that's all she said. She didn't point out the false equivalences, that this was a major life-altering upheaval, not summer camp. He was trying, and right now that mattered.

But what also mattered this instant was that she could not allow him to come inside her cottage where Bloc was likely still spread open-legged on her air mattress. She squeezed his arm. "Okay, so maybe I won't make good on my threat and leave you on the side of the road. If we were in Philly right now, I might consider it, but these exurbs out here are where racists rule."

He chuckled. "Well, that's a relief. I guess I owe the racists one."

"And furthermore, just drop me at my door and head on home."

"But I wanted to peep in and see it with furniture."

"Absolutely not! I guarantee you you'll have suggestion after suggestion and before you know it, it will be completely dark, bewitching hour for a Black man driving a car like yours on these dark roads with these shoot-first, ask-questions-later backwoods cops. Anyhow, I haven't even scheduled the people who'll come to help me situate things so there's nothing to even see. Now, goodbye, be gone, my child. Really, I don't want to have to be holding your picture and sobbing at a Black Lives Matter demonstration."

"You do know such a thing could happen as easily in Philly?"

"But they'll get away with it easier out here."

"Yes, Mother," he said, as he pulled in front of her cottage and leaned over and kissed her forehead.

"Email me the details of the offer and we'll talk in the morning." She was out of the car when he rolled down his window and called out to her and she was already prepared with another reason for why he couldn't come in.

"I do know this is hard for you, Mom. Just, you know, be open to letting things settle in. They will."

She blew him a kiss. "Hug Melanie for me. And text me when you're in safe and sound."

He nodded and waved and she watched him drive around the circle under the canopy formed by the leafed-out oak and maple trees. Such stunning trees. The only reason she'd even gotten out of the car when E had coerced her here to see the decorated cottage had been the trees. She wished they'd planted saplings instead as E's car disappeared around the loop.

She opened the door to her cottage. The sky was red and blue falling in through the skylight and cast a purple haze over the sleeping giant still on the air mattress. Her breath caught in her throat as she considered that she'd lived here for a single night and day and had already slept with a man about whom she knew very little. He appeared kingly under the purple hue and Cynthia convinced herself that she knew enough about him: knew that his laugh was genuine; his eyes went soft when he spoke of his children; he'd waited for her to make the first move.

She lifted her quilt from the orange corduroy chair and eased onto the mattress and covered them both. She laid her head on his shoulder and he sputtered awake. "Hey, foxy lady, you back," he said in a groggy voice.

"Foxy lady? What you do, forget my name?"

"Your name? I don't remember my own name. That was some good shit we smoked. I do remember that."

"It was," Cynthia said, as she watched her tears falling onto his shoulder.

"Whoa. What's going on?" he asked, as he wrapped his other arm around her and squeezed her to him.

"I want to go home, I want to be back in my own house. You know. And I was thinking my house would always be there for me to return to but someone just made an offer—"

"Well, that's a relief," he said as he patted her back.

"Relief, no, it's devastating," she said, her voice rising.

"I know, I know," he whispered. "Forgive me for making it

about me, but I thought you might be crying because you looked at me all up here in your great room, and you said to yourself, what the eff did I just do, let me get the hell out of here and go back home, oh wait, this is home."

"Well, there's that, too," she said, feeling a glimmer of a laugh trying to break through.

He did laugh as he rubbed her back. "Trust me, pretty lady, it gets better. You'll let go of what you've left, and you'll replace it a little at a time by what you find here. It takes time, but I promise you it gets better."

She couldn't remember the last time she'd felt so comforted by a man. She didn't try to count back. She nestled into his warmth instead.

Three

Cynthia felt especially pretty now as she walked Bloc to the door. She reasoned that the act of allowing her desires to percolate through the entirety of her womanhood yesterday and expressing that womanhood had rearranged her, softened her features, and lifted her breasts, and unkinked the very tight muscles in her lower back. She felt like a version of the Tin Man who just got some oil as she and Bloc lingered at her doorway and he kissed her mouth again and again. He whispered that just in case he'd dreamed the previous day into this morning, he wanted to stretch the dream for as long as he could. She laughed and pushed him away, playfully, then cleared her throat and asked him if he was planning to go to Tish's later, Tish had invited her during the reception yesterday so she just wanted to know if he would be there too. She noticed the muscles in his face tighten as he said that he had some early errands, then a visit with his daughter and grandchildren in the afternoon in downtown Philly. So it depended, he said, on how long that visit lasted, and whether or not his grandchildren managed to convince him to spend the night. Then he kissed her again, letting his lips brush back and forth against her mouth. She gave in to the feel of his lips, even though she wanted to ask him if there was anything she needed to know, did he and Tish have something going on. She'd not asked him yesterday for fear that his response might have caused her to withhold her needy hands from his urgent, inflated manhood. She thought that his reaction just now, his clenched jaw, expressed everything she didn't want to know. She stood at the door and watched him walk away into the mist rising from the grass as if the earth were sighing on her behalf, pushing up moistened breath that glistened like silver dust.

. . .

Bloc was sighing, too, as he walked back to his cottage and felt the morning air moving through the transplanted trees like finger wags. He was doing it again: sabotaging a relationship. He'd been doing it since he was a teen and the mothers of the cute West Philly girls pushed their daughters in Bloc's direction because he was smart and had future earning potential. He'd take one to Dewey's for burgers and cherry Cokes and become mesmerized by the cleft in her chin, or the perfect curve to her bangs, or the way she tilted her head as if not to disturb the crown she wore because she was a princess and knew it. "Can I stand a chance with you?" he'd ask, enraptured by the spectacle of adolescent loveliness sitting across from him using her fork to eat her fries even as he lifted his with his fingers. He'd taste the nitrogen in the clouds as he floated home. She was more than he could ever want, until the following month when he wanted even more.

Enter the next cute girl he'd take to Horn & Hardart where he'd treat her to Salisbury steak, mashed potatoes, and tapioca that was fresh from the automat in those scallop-edge dessert glasses, decorative cinnamon sticks plunging into the pudding's sweet thickness. He'd fall in love with the single dimple in her cheek and the eyes that curved downward like cashews, infatuation over last month's chin cleft and perfectly turned bangs already forgotten. The proclivity followed him through high school, college, graduate school, one, two wives. Though he met his match with the third wife, who'd demolished him.

He considered therapy after that one. But he'd always likened the psychotherapeutic process to trying to scratch a back itch that is hard to reach, when finally, the fingers get at the itch right at the center to much relief, until the spot next to it clamors for attention, and the one next to that, the one above, below, until the entire back becomes a screaming siren, a welted, blistered mess, with no way to relieve the cacophony that's been unleashed. He reasoned that a therapist would only point out what he already knew, that he was merely playing catch-up because he wasn't always considered brilliant. Just the opposite.

His nickname had actually been Blockhead because he was severely nearsighted as a child and would tilt his head and squint when spoken to so everyone assumed that he was slow to comprehend. His mother's boss was the first to figure out the truth.

Bloc's mother had worked at Scotty's Hoagie and Variety, the corner store that sold everything from penny candy, to discs for playing 45s, to cheesesteaks, to Olivo hair pomade, to peanuts roasted under a hot light, to black-and-white composition books and number two pencils, to pickled pigs' feet in a big glass jar. His mother, Maryann, was Scott's human cash register. No matter the conglomeration of items a person bought, Scott would call out the price of each item to Maryann and she'd do the addition in her head and give him the total; he'd say how much money the customer presented; she'd tell him how much change they should get back. She was quick with it. So quick that some customers used a pencil and paper to check her math. She'd never erred.

Bloc was proud of his mother's genius. He'd meet her at Scotty's to walk home with her each day at exactly 4:07, no matter what he was doing: he might be sitting very close to the television watching *Chief Halftown* or *Popeye Theater*; he might be playing hide-and-seek up and down the back alleys that smelled of apple blossoms and cat urine; he might be walking Shelly, the beautiful lab belonging to Mr. Rochester—Rochester worked nights at the post office and paid Bloc two dollars and fifty cents a week for walking his dog. Whatever he was doing, he'd disentangle himself so that he could descend into the basement corner store at exactly 4:07, squinting, and grinning because his mother's face was like sunshine to him.

On the day Bloc discovered that he did not lack comprehension skills, he'd just left Rochester with the steam still rising from his skin. He'd never been so close to Rochester before where he could actually feel the cloud of heat and moisture surrounding him. Rochester always seemed to just be exiting the shower when Bloc returned Shelly, and ordinarily Bloc would open the door wide enough for Shelly to get back in the house and even though Rochester would be standing in the middle of the living room dripping and naked, Bloc was unaffected because with his near-sightedness, Rochester was totally nonthreatening, just a pear-shaped blob the color of a chocolate-and-strawberry milkshake blended well. Plus, Bloc had never really had to enter the guts of the living room. Shelly always waited for Bloc by the front door panting, tail wagging, so all Bloc had to do was barely open the door and Shelly was squeezing through onto the porch, jumping on Bloc as if to give him a hug. But this day when Bloc returned with Shelly and opened the door and motioned her in, Rochester called his name. "Blankwood, I want to ask you something," he said. His voice sounded official like a television announcer saying that *Lassie* would not be shown because of a special news update. Bloc stepped all the way into the living room, which was unnaturally dark the way that rooms are when the blinds are closed tightly on a bright day. "Help me dry off," Rochester said.

"I don't want to," Bloc said, as he started backing up toward the door. He could hear Shelly's heavy breathing and he looked at her rather than the rotund mass approaching him. Shelly's head was tilted as if she was confused as Rochester grabbed Bloc's arm and pulled him so close that Bloc could actually discern the features on Rochester's face with its flaring nose and desperate bones that formed the sockets under his eyes.

Bloc tried to wrench his arm away. He tussled with Rochester in the middle of the living room as remnants of shower water left blotches on the hardwood floor. "Leave me alone, I wanna go," Bloc cried. Shelly, not knowing whose side to take, whimpered and then released a high-pitched half bark and threw herself between them, allowing Bloc to break free. He ran from the house thinking about how much he loved that dog.

Then at 4:07, like he'd done every day from the time he was eight, he walked into Scott's Hoagie and Variety and there was his mother sitting at the counter, her lavender-colored sweater over her shoulders, her black patent leather purse hanging from her arm. "There's my best boy," she said, like she always said when he walked into the store.

"Well, tell me this," Scott asked, as he came from behind the counter smelling of dill pickles and bologna. Bloc's breath caught in his throat as he wondered if Scott somehow knew what had just happened in Mr. Rochester's living room; Scott might even blame him, accuse him of doing something to make Rochester come after him like he'd done. He wondered if he had done something. "What kinda watch you wear?" Scott finished his question and Bloc let go of his pent-up breath.

"I don't have a watch," he answered.

"Well, how you get here the same time every day, to the second, 'cause I done took note of it."

"I know the time by what the sun does."

"Well, how you explain it when it's raining?"

"The light still looks a certain way."

"Well, whatcho do when the seasons change?"

"I know how the light moves?"

"How do it?"

Bloc made a protractor with his fingers. He put his index

finger against the cracked leather stool next to the one where his mother sat. He walked his second finger around in a slow circle as he explained where the light was at 4:07 on Christmas Eve, versus where it was on his birthday the second week in April. "And that's it, that's how I know," Bloc said, looking at the pattern of oil splotches on Scotty's apron.

"That's it?" Scotty asked, running his fingers through his hair that was red from overprocessing.

"Well, that plus what I feel on the inside that tells me, like in my chest."

"Your chest? You're not wheezing, are you?" his mother asked.

"Maryann, the boy's a genius. I'm telling you what I know," Scotty said. "He figured out how to track the sun with his mind and then his intuition let him know he hit the nail on the head. That's the mark of an Einstein."

Bloc turned to look at his mother, her expression caught between amazement and concern; he was close enough to practically see the crease in her forehead that her barrel-shaped bang almost hid. Every Saturday morning she got her hair done across the street at Miss C's Beauty Salon. Bloc always offered her half of what he earned walking Shelly. She always declined, but he loved the way the gesture made him feel. He was due to be paid tomorrow. A shrill feeling moved through his stomach as he worried that his envelope would not be resting in the empty planter that sat in the far corner of Mr. Rochester's porch. He steadied himself against the threat of nausea over the thought of going into that darkened living room to demand his wages.

"Well, of course I think he's a genius." His mother leaned down and smooched his cheek. "But they're talking about holding him back and making him repeat fourth grade—"

"That's 'cause they the ones can't comprehend. They presented with a brain the likes of the one this boy got, and all they can do is say he's slow. Shameful the way they do little colored kids. They'd a sent a white kid to Harvard." Scotty went behind the counter and pointed to a sign high on the wall above the shelf that held Jiffy Shoe Polish, twelve-to-a-pack wooden clothespins, and Glover's Mange hair treatment. "Read what that says."

Bloc squinted, seeing nothing but indecipherable strokes from where he sat. "Uh, I can't?" he more asked than answered.

"He needs remedial reading," his mother said.

"Naw, naw, naw," Scotty said as he grabbed the pole for reaching high places and clipped it onto the sign and deftly eased the sign from the shelf. He pushed the sign right at Bloc's face. "What it say now?"

"In God we trust, all others pay cash," Bloc read easily.

His mother squealed and clapped and Scotty laughed, pleased with himself. "Maryann, this boy don't need remedial nothing, he just needs glasses. You take him to get his vision fixed. I'll cover the price. And, Bloc, you pick out anything you want from this store, right here and now, just consider it my down payment on your success."

Bloc picked out a switchblade. Scotty showed him where to press to make the blade jump out and Bloc was mesmerized by the blade, how sharp it was, how neatly it fit back into its compartment, tucked out of view. He likened it to his just-discovered expansive mental capacity. Hidden away at first, dumb boy, dumb boy, dumbass boy. But then the right spot was touched and out of nowhere, Zam! Cut, puncture, stab, through the lung, through the heart, going for the kill. *Take that and that and that, Mr. Rochester. And more than that even if you don't have the money I rightfully earned walking that beautiful dog that you hardly deserve 'cause I'm nobody's fool.*

. . .

That Bloc was nobody's fool became apparent when he could see the chalkboard from the back of the classroom and confidently raise his hand and proclaim the answer to arithmetic questions. He won ribbons at science fairs, amassed checkmarks under the Outstanding column on report card after report card. He ferried invitations to play with the kids from the better homes. And then, despite his shiny skin and thick-lensed glasses, the smiles from girls began. So many girls. It was impossible to choose just one.

Four

After Bloc disappeared into the mist, Cynthia wanted more than anything to talk to Gabriella. She hunted for her phone and found it atop a box of unpacked kitchen items she'd been using as a coffee table. She smiled when she saw a text from Gabriella glowing on her phone saying that she had the triplets for the weekend so she would call when they weren't eating or fighting or shitting themselves, or otherwise commanding her attention by being absolutely adorable. But in the meantime she wanted to know if she was feeling less homesick at that Sexagenarian, and by the way, did she think there would be any sex to be had there?

Cynthia laughed as she typed out her reply. *Gab, for full effect, read this to the tune of KC and the Sunshine Band: smoked a little weed, made a little love, got down last night, whoo, got down last night. Got down, got down, got down got down got down last night, baaaby.* She sang the song herself as she laughed through her shower and while she dressed. Laughed more when she saw Gabriella's reply, popped-eye emoji followed by, *Gurrl! Calling you first chance I get.*

She made a cup of tea and sat at her counter and looked out

on her great room where she and Bloc's love den of an air mattress was still spread. She planned her strategy for unpacking. She'd pace herself. She'd also have to think about what she'd wear to Tish's tonight—she could tell that Tish was a fashionista—then said to herself, so what, she wasn't in competition with Tish; she hadn't dressed based on someone's else barometer since at least college, then corrected herself, since high school, because in college it was all about faded jeans and wide belts with buckles made of peace sign medallions. She shook the thought of peace sign belt buckles lest she descend into thoughts of Mr. Z, the married man she'd been with in college who had worn such a belt. Cynthia thought that he had sported that belt to prove that he was hip, down, even though he was old enough to be somebody's father. Now she was hearing the clanging sounds the belt made as it tapped the metal sides of her dorm room bed.

This is how it always happened. When Cynthia's attention was drawn to immediate concerns, as it was now with the move and Bloc and going to Tish's and letting go of her house, a piece of Mr. Z would escape from where she had pouched him under years of intentional forgetting, allowing him to sneak into her conscious mind. In her three-story house with its plethora of hiding places, she could stuff away first thoughts of him before the pieces could form the whole of him that would wreck her the way he had wrecked her that night. Here there were no cobwebbed attics, or mothball-infused storage closets, or enter-if-you-dare crawl spaces. Here there was just one expansive floor of openness gushing light and air. Here there was new soft soil that would float everything to the surface.

She was in a danger zone here. Cynthia pushed the lever to deflate the air mattress. She watched the mattress relinquish its suppleness and transform into an airless version of itself. She concentrated on the hissing sounds the mattress made to override the sound in her head of metal on metal. But now she was seeing his smile.

She tried to shut down the image of his smile by stuffing the deflated air mattress into its covering, then pounding it into its box. She kicked the box into the bottom of the closet. Now she was remembering how Gabriella had laughed in her ear after Mr. Z's smile. It was safer to think about Gabriella.

"Damn, girl. What we got going here?" Gabriella had whispered. Cynthia hunched her shoulders in response, faking ignorance.

"You are aware that's a come-on smile."

"Please," Cynthia said, as she leaned down to push her book bag under her seat, feeling that familiar regret rise in her chest if a man came on to her, thinking that once he saw her close-up he'd be disappointed.

"Cynt, the man thinks you're gorgeous; you're the only one who doesn't realize it," Gabriella said. Cynthia and Gabriella were girls. Where one faltered, the other bolstered.

• • •

They'd met during their teen years when they attended the same, but different high schools. The building was cordoned off so that one side housed classes for the college-bound smart kids such as Cynthia, and the other for average and/or underperforming students.

It was the beginning of the school year and Cynthia had already tired of her classmates' between-period banter about their mothers: *my mom said chesterfield coats are all the go this season; my mom found me the cutest textured stockings on sale at Lit Brothers; my mom gonna be my Girl Scout troop's cookie mother this year so I'm gonna be eating Thin Mints nonstop.* There was nothing Cynthia could add to such dialogues since she didn't have that type of mother. Although a part of her wanted to blurt out, *My mom's man this week was tall and dark as Sidney Poitier and for your information, Darlene, he looked a lot like your dad who has the nerve to be chairman of the deacon board. And her man last week had a limp just like Bernadette's father, though last month's man, 'cause he came around for a full thirty days so I got to see his face often with that god-awful mole on the tip of his nose, was definitely your dad, Lisa. I'm sure your mom must have wondered where he was all those nights.* Though as much as she wanted to wrestle the narrative away from them, humiliate a few of them the way they constantly did her, she wasn't that bold.

On the day Cynthia met Gabriella, she'd ventured to the side of the school to use the bathroom where the nonelite students were. She'd just left geometry class where she'd raised her hand to answer a question about the base of an equilateral triangle and was certain she heard someone whisper that it was the distance between her mom's knees when her legs are spread.

It was darker on the other side of the building, light bulbs missing from what had once been a grand chandelier in the main corridor. Paint chipped from the walls; the floors lacked the buffed-up shine Cynthia was used to on her side. But it was thrilling, too, as she pushed through a cloud of cigarette smoke to get into the girls' bathroom where the laughter was raucous, and for once she was sure they were not laughing about her because she was an unknown on that side of the building. A transistor radio blared Martha and the Vandellas singing "Dancing in the Street," and then the bathroom erupted with the sounds of everyone shouting the part about Philadelphia, PA. They laughed and slapped hands and the bell sounded and most left, though Cynthia lingered, captivated by the unbound energy in there.

Gabriella leaned against the sink smoking a cigarette. She was tall and poised in a tartan plaid pleated skirt and bright yellow turtleneck that complemented her complexion, which was coppery gold. Her knee socks matched the turtleneck and her bronze-colored loafers sported pennies in the slits. She wore her hair pulled back in an off-centered bun, slicked with gel so the waves showed. Her earrings were oversize hoops; her lipstick the richest shade Cynthia had ever seen, mocha berry. Cynthia knew because she searched McCrory's, and Green's and Woolworth's that following weekend until she finally found it at the makeup counter at Gimbels. The lipstick stained the Kool filter tip cigarette that Gabriella was smoking and Cynthia asked her if she could get a catch off the cigarette, the way she'd hear her mother occasionally ask her company. Gabriella looked Cynthia up and down, but not in the judgmental way the girls on the other side of the building did. It was more of an assessment. She handed Cynthia the cigarette and then asked her if she even knew how to smoke.

"You tell me," Cynthia said, as she took a puff and blew it out without inhaling.

Gabriella laughed. "You cute."

"I look okay."

"Better than okay," Gabriella said, as she took the cigarette from Cynthia and drew in hard. "Your look is awkward right now, but you gonna be really pretty once your eyes and mouth catch up with your nose."

"How you know?" Cynthia asked with a smirk.

"I know faces, that's how I know. I can draw a face I've only seen once maybe years ago. And I can also predict how someone's face will change over time. My uncle is a detective and he says I'm gifted and he can get me a job as a sketch artist with the courts once I graduate high school. So yeah, that's how I know," she said emphatically, as Cynthia reached for the cigarette again and Gabriella waved her hand away. "And I also know you best get your butt over to the other side of the building. We can do whatever we want over here; if it wasn't for Mom and uncles demanding my excellence, I could cut class all day long. But the teachers on your side of the building pay attention to y'all so you should do it for all it's worth."

Cynthia returned to the exhilarating dankness of the other side of the building the next week, the mocha berry color swathed over her lips. She pushed into the bathroom alive with chatter and profanity and a trio of girls singing "To Sir, With Love," then laughing when two of them couldn't hit the high note. Gabriella sat on the floor, her book bag as a pillow. She read from her three-ring binder, closed her eyes and mouthed some words, then started reading again. Cynthia cleared her throat and said, "Hi, Gabriella, what you up to."

Gabriella held her hand up like a stop sign, said, "Not now, please, I'm cramming for a quiz next period." She looked up and saw Cynthia, and the irritation on her face ebbed into a smile.

"Look at you in your lipstick; you gotta learn how to swab, though, but right now I don't have time to teach you." Then she focused on her binder again and Cynthia left the bathroom feeling a mix of dejection and elation and wondered why Gabriella hadn't gone to the library to study, until she discovered that that side of the building had no library. She felt sorry for Gabriella and the girls who had been singing "To Sir, With Love," and the ones cursing and talking in the loudest of voices. She felt envy, too, that they'd found comradery and security in that dismal bathroom that smelled of barbecue potato chips and cigarette smoke, and where the air wept with frivolity and joy. It was intoxicating and Cynthia was drawn there again and again during her free periods where she'd otherwise be alone on her side of the building trying to avoid the tee-hees of her classmates as they chattered about the superficialities of their lives.

Gabriella became as frequent a visitor to Cynthia's cafeteria as Cynthia was to Gabriella's haven of a bathroom. Gabriella would sketch the faces of Cynthia's classmates and adorn them with devil's ears or Medusa-like hair to make Cynthia laugh. Cynthia was astounded at the accuracy of Gabriella's renderings and she would push Gabriella to consider college. She wanted that as much for herself as for Gabriella so that their classes could be on the same side of the building. Internally bound by nature,

Cynthia was exuberant when she was with Gabriella. She especially loved going home with her. Outside Cynthia's grandmother's house, and occasionally church when the good choir sang with their clap-to rhythms, the only other place Cynthia felt so entirely unfettered was at Gabriella's house. She laughed from a new place when she was there. Gabriella's uncles, Hal the preacher, Don the bartender, and Nathan the police detective, were always dropping by and entertaining them with stories of bringing someone to joy: the joy of gin and tonic, the joy of justice, the joy of Jesus. Gabriella's mother, Cassie, was an operator at Bell Telephone Company and would have them hysterical as she imitated the voices she'd hear in the course of a day.

The first time Cynthia went to Gabriella's house, Gabriella pulled her into the kitchen where Cassie was forming salmon into plump patties stuffed with green peppers and onions, rice and corn, and dropping them into a skillet. "Mom, Mom," Gabriella called urgently, "this is Cynthia, how beautiful is she?"

"Well, let me turn around and I'll tell you," Cassie said, as she pushed her hands under the faucet to clean them. Cassie was a slightly older Gabriella with the same coppery-colored skin and crinkly hair and big eyes that turned down at the corners. Her hands were damp but warm when she cupped them around Cynthia's cheeks and said, "Gab's right, you are absolutely beautiful. And more than that, you've got a beautiful spirit. Gab knows faces, but I know hearts."

"What kind of heart does she have, Mom?" Gabriella asked, as she stood next to her mother and bounced excitedly.

Cassie hesitated as she studied Cynthia's face, then she pulled

Cynthia into a hug and said, "A really large and generous heart that deserves all the love."

Gabriella's house felt enormous to Cynthia, though it was no larger than her own house, or her grandmother's. The emotional square footage there accommodated any arrangement of moods or fits or hilarity with acres left over to still move around, not compressed like it was at Cynthia's house where she squeezed herself into a corner because her mother's behavior took up all the space, all the air. She'd marvel at Gabriella's ability to have an outburst in front of her mother, slam her books on the table, and it was okay. Okay! At such times she'd wish Cassie, not Divine, was her mother. Later, when she was back at her own house, her feelings stuffed into the minuscule space allotted her at home—likely after Divine had tempted some random man with that rapturous smile of hers, lowered eye, pursed lip, face-flushed-with-desire look; that look that was the prelude to the after-dark rings of the doorbell, the hushed giggles in the kitchen, the furtive press of feet on the stairs, the moan of air as the bedroom door sealed shut and Cynthia would listen for the reverse as Divine escorted her company back out—Cynthia would wait for her mother at the top of the stairs. "I can't sleep, will you stay in my bed?" she'd ask Divine, who'd always reply, "Well, of course, silly, what good is a mommy who can't put her baby to sleep"; they'd curl up and fit together like the two last pieces in a jigsaw puzzle snapping into place: Cynthia would feel guilty then for wishing that Cassie was her mother, especially as she felt the protrusion of bones in Divine's back and was reminded how frail she was.

She felt guilty, too, for keeping her mother hidden from Gabriella, believing that was the reason for their unencumbered friendship. She'd invite Gabriella to her grandmother's house instead. They'd sip tea from Rose's china cups and laugh at Rose's commentary as she talked back to the people on her soap operas. Gabriella and Rose bonded so that before long Gabriella was calling Rose Gramum just like Cynthia did. Cynthia was relieved that Gabriella never asked about Divine. Though she would come to realize years later that Gabriella had known about Divine all along.

Gabriella's uncle Nathan, the police detective, had dated Divine several years ago. He'd fallen in love and Divine professed the same. She couldn't not be with other men, though, and it broke Nathan. "It got to the point where she just didn't even care anymore," he confessed to Gabriella and Cassie and his brothers. "And I was, like, got damn, she gonna make me kill some cat out here, and it's not like I'm a white boy and could get away with it. I'd be out of a job, and behind bars my damned self for wrongful discharge of a firearm." He told them that the worst part was that Divine had a nice little studious daughter who seemed to stay away from the house as much as she could and practically lived with her grandmother.

So Gabriella's heart had gone soft for Cynthia before they ever met in that school bathroom. Gabriella's own mother was her sun and stars and moon combined. And the way her mother's three older brothers doted on her, Gabriella knew that she was the center of their world. She could not fathom Cynthia's life. After Gabriella shooed Cynthia from the bathroom that first day they'd met, and one of the girls told Gabriella who Cynthia's mother was, Gabriella said, "So what the hell. She's my new friend and I trust y'all to treat her right."

That's the kind of friend Gabriella was.

• • •

Cynthia walked through the great room preparing to begin tackling the taped boxes. She was facing the floor-to-ceiling window that looked out on the front of her cottage, then said to herself, *You've got to be kidding me.* Her son and daughter-in-law were walking toward her door and she realized she'd escaped a catastrophe in that they hadn't shown up a half hour earlier when she and Bloc were sleeping tangled on the air mattress. She felt a mix of joy and dread: joy because they were at the center of what made her truly happy, watching them prosper, not just financially, but as decent human beings bettering themselves through the daily churn of turning lumps of curd into butter; dread because they were exhausting, since they knew everything and she knew nothing.

She faulted herself. When E was a little boy, Cynthia would pretend ignorance so that he could wrestle with a problem, solve it, and then teach her. She thought it made him trust his own abilities. The downside was that he seemed never to have figured out that she knew some things. And he'd married his double as far as that went, both self-assured lawyers with strong opinions and sunny dispositions. They even looked alike with their reddened complexions and soft dark eyes and thick curly hair, though Melanie wore hers flat ironed. This morning, though, Melanie's hair was pulled up in a righteous ponytail, signaling that she came to work.

Melanie did work; E did, too. Cynthia thought that they plowed through her unpacking better than the people the development paid to do such things. E even went over to maintenance and borrowed tools and put her bed together.

By late afternoon Cynthia tried to hurry them along. She needed for them to leave, needed to watch the back of their car go around the curve toward the development's exit because she wanted time to prepare herself for the gathering at Tish's; she wanted to twist her hair to stretch out her 'fro, wanted to figure out what she would wear, and mostly she wanted time to manage her anxiety, maybe do a meditation, a couple of yoga poses. She regretted now that she'd not gotten clarification about the nature of Bloc's relationship with Tish before he left this morning, even as she felt silly for being anxious. She felt like a teenager on her way to a party where the boy she liked may or may not be there, and the host may or may not be his girlfriend.

"What is this monstrosity?" Melanie asked as she unwrapped a glass chia-type figurine with wild hair and oversize eyes.

"Mine," Cynthia said, as she grabbed it from Melanie, then apologized for snatching it from her. "It's from Gabriella so it's special, ugly but special," she said, as she held it up to the light. Gabriella had given the figurine to Cynthia when Cynthia first learned of Ethrow's affair. Gabriella fashioned herself a witch by then and told Cynthia to make nice with the woman and give her the figurine as a gift. She promised it would not bring the woman harm, it would just turn off the attraction she had for Ethrow, adding that Ethrow should be glad that she was a good witch 'cause otherwise she would have worked a spell to make his dick fall off. Cynthia had laughed so hard until she cried when Gabriella said that, and then she did cry, not because of the affair, but because she realized Ethrow wasn't even worth that much effort anymore.

"Speaking of ugly," Melanie said, as she pointed to the orange corduroy swivel chair.

"Leave my chair alone, Melanie," Cynthia said, as she remembered how when she and Bloc were looking for a place to lie and he asked her where had she slept the past two nights, she pointed to that chair. And then how they'd laughed as they watched the air mattress inflate and Cynthia had said, *It's imitating you during the reception.*

She held her laughter now as she listened to Melanie clear her throat lest she ask Cynthia what was so funny.

"So about the chair, Mom," Melanie said.

"Not listening, Melanie," Cynthia said, as she rewrapped the figurine in tissue paper as Melanie snapped pictures of the chair.

"So, Mom, really, nothing against the chair, but it's just that in your old house, okay, maybe the chair fit, you know, the house was a classic colonial, and the chair is so, so vintage, but here, well, it's so out of context here, especially in its current condition."

"I'd say the chair and I have a lot in common then. I'm keeping the chair, Melanie," Cynthia said, as she went into the bedroom to see how E was making out.

E had the bed put together and Cynthia told him where to position it, then Melanie came in the room squealing that her friend Jen restored vintage furniture, and was familiar with that orange swivel chair and had just texted her tons of swatches, and was certain that she could restore the chair and make it beautiful again.

"I like the chair the way it is, Melanie," Cynthia said, as she swallowed the impulse to say more.

"No, Mom, the bed can't stay like this," Melanie said, having moved on from the chair.

"I was thinking the same thing," E said, as he went to stand next to Melanie and kissed her shoulder, and Cynthia thought about what beautiful grandchildren they'd give her and wished they would hurry up so they could focus on someone who really needed their attention.

"Okay, I hate to ask, but what's wrong with the bed?"

"Well, the back of it really shouldn't face the door," E said.

"Yeah, turn it around, sweetie," Melanie said.

Cynthia held up her hand, told them that she wanted the bed right where it was.

"Can I ask why?" Melanie asked.

"Because I want to watch the sun rise from the bed."

"But, Mom," E said, "the trees will block that anyhow."

"You are so right, sweetie," Melanie agreed.

Cynthia countered, "Nothing can block the streams of light that cut a path through the trees and go from blue to pink to yellow, and I can even spot rainbows if the mist is hanging just right. And regardless, it will be fall soon enough; the leaves will be gone, and I'll have a front row seat to the majesty of daybreak as the sun explodes from the night right before my eyes."

They were both quiet then and Cynthia congratulated herself. But then Melanie cleared her throat, said, "So, Mom, that's beautiful, it really is, I mean you have such a way with words, but may I just point out that since there are windows everywhere in the bedroom, all you have to do is step out of bed and turn around."

"My dear, I am not thirty-five, okay. I do ten minutes of gentle bed stretching before my feet even hit the floor—"

"Oh my god, Mom," Melanie interrupted, "please don't tell me you stretch cold muscles, that can be so, so dangerous—"

"I toss and turn a lot, so they're lukewarm by the time I wake," Cynthia said, "but whatever, I want my bed where I want it, thank you."

"Well, all right then, but I just feel bad that the feng shui is all wrong with the back of the bed facing the door," Melanie said.

"Right?" E agreed. And Cynthia picked up a pillow and punched it really hard, punching back her urge to say, *Fuck feng shui.*

Before they prepared to leave, finally, they programmed Cynthia's refrigerator. Cynthia stressed that all she wanted to order automatically was half-and-half. E suggested that she could have butter and eggs also automatically ordered. Melanie pointed out that the sensors in the crisper meant that she could do the same with broccoli, lettuce, tomatoes—

"Stop it," Cynthia said. "Not eggs, not butter, not broccoli or whatever the fuck. Okay, the only thing I'll miss if I run out of it is the half-and-half, just the motherfucking half-and-half, okay."

E and Melanie looked as if they'd been slapped. Then E squeezed Melanie's shoulder. "Let's go, babe," he said.

"I'm so ready, sweetie," Melanie said, looking down so she didn't have to look at Cynthia.

Cynthia watched E and Melanie as they headed for the door, their shoulders hunched in identical ways, signaling how upset they were. She couldn't let them leave while they were upset with her. She was superstitious that way.

"Wait," she called, as she rushed to them and apologized for her language and for yelling. "All this moving and unpacking has me so stressed out. Please forgive me." She kissed both their cheeks. Asked them to let her make it up to them by treating them to a meal at the Throwback, the burger joint at the Shops at the Sexagenarian where they could get a real burger and shake, or a vegan variety and a fruit smoothie. They agreed.

. . .

The Throwback was alive with sounds. The jukebox pushed out Alicia Keys; chatter floated from the other booths; the servers chirped the specials for the day; the smoothie maker whirled and buzzed; forks tinged plates; the short order cook called out, "my man pots and pans." And E and Melanie were back to their effusive selves, to Cynthia's relief. They fell into easy conversation with the several people who paused at the booth to welcome Cynthia again to the Gen. There was Judith, the Dolly Parton look-alike who invited Cynthia to join her next month at the Climate March; Cornelius, the committee person, who asked her to help him canvass for the midterms; Bobbi, who used to be Robert, a retired chemistry teacher who now did stand-up and who performed a miniroutine at their table about trying to convince herself that the Throwback's vegan milkshakes were the real thing.

Then Maze and her husband, Roy, came over to the table. Roy peppered E and Melanie with questions about what they did, where they'd gone to law school, undergrad. Maze interrupted him, "Before he asks about your pre-K experience, we're going to let you guys eat, and go get a booth for ourselves." Laughter around until they were out of earshot and Melanie remarked how engaging everyone here seemed to be, especially Maze.

"I really like Maze," Cynthia said. "We chatted yesterday at the reception; she's a retired public defender."

"Well, of course she is," Melanie said. "I bet she really cared about her clients too. She exudes empathy."

"But I'm willing to bet her husband was nobody's public defender," E said.

"You would be right. He was a judge," Cynthia said, leaning in and whispering.

"Oh my god, such an odd pairing," Melanie said, as she bit into her mushroom and spinach sandwich leaking pepper jack cheese. "Maze in her mismatched feather earrings and flower-child dress and rocking her white-girl 'fro, and Roy in his blue blazer and yacht loafers."

"And his interrogations," E said, as he touched the tip of his napkin against Melanie's chin to wipe away the cheese.

"You felt it too, right, babe?" Melanie said. "So E and I talk about this all the time, Mom, how some white people are quick to ask you what do you do, before they even ask your name. You know, where are you from, where'd you go to school, summer camp? On and on. But we've gotten really good at differentiating between those who really want to get to know us, and those who mainly want to know how we qualify to be in the same room with them."

"That would be Roy," Cynthia said. "I understand that when he moved in, he mistook the only Black man who lives here for the porter." Tish had told her that at the reception yesterday as she'd whispered to Cynthia tidbits about who was who.

"That's just awful," E said.

"Wait, a Black man lives here?" Melanie asked.

"Yeah, just the one," Cynthia said, trying to sound as non-chalant as she could.

"Are there many single men here? And what about him, is he a solo act, or living with a she, he, or they?"

"Far as I know, just him, but I don't know too far." Cynthia sipped her smoothie.

"Well, have you met him? What's he like?" Melanie asked.

"Nice enough, I guess, too nice for some white man to be demanding that he get his bags from his trunk. The thought of it makes me want to curse."

"And we know you know how to curse," E said, teasingly. Cynthia sensed that E was as eager as she was to turn the conversation from where Melanie was trying to take it.

"How about Mom a little bit ago, Melanie." E laughed, as he commenced to imitate Cynthia. "'Hands off my refrigerator and get the eff out of my house.'"

"I did not tell you to get out," she said, as she settled deeper into the softness of the booth, enjoying their playful back-and-forth.

"I have to say, Mom, I haven't heard you use language like that since you were in the hospital," Melanie said. "You were having some serious arguments in your dreams from that hospital bed. Cursing about— Who was it, babe?"

"Mr. Z," E said.

"Right, Mr. Z. Oh my god, Mom, E was getting upset because you were like fighting this Mr. Z in your mostly unconscious state." She rubbed E's back as she talked. "But we knew you were coming around when you started settling down. And then no more mention of him."

"Thank god," E said. "I was wondering who the heck that guy is, anyhow."

"Yeah, who is Mr. Z, Mom?"

An unhappy baby began to howl, overtaking the Throwback's other sounds, the chatter and the laughter and the beats thumping from the jukebox, and E and Melanie repeating Mr. Z, over and over until they were shouting his name. Though they weren't really repeating, shouting his name. But that's all Cynthia heard as she grabbed for the other sounds as if the other sounds were crags along a mountainside that she could use to hoist herself up, to hold on to, to prevent her descent into the rapids below.

Five

His name wasn't really Mr. Z. His name was really Gordon Willis. Gabriella invented the name Mr. Z for him so they never had to give breath to his real name, so that no one would ever know what happened that night. And now Cynthia had just learned that she'd said his name out loud to someone other than Gabriella. Even though it wasn't his actual name, it still represented him. And hearing that aural representation of him from E and Melanie paralyzed her for several seconds, long enough for E to ask if she was okay. She blamed her reaction on brain freeze from the smoothie, then said that was her cue that it was time for coffee. She signaled the server so that she could order a cup of half decaf, half regular, and managed to deflect talk of Mr. Z as she asked E and Melanie about their plans to sell their condo and buy a house.

Now Cynthia was back at her cottage unzipping garment bags as she pondered what to wear to Tish's. She tried to hold at bay any thought of Mr. Z. Though she knew too well that trying not to think of a thing made that very thing move through her head like a sloth, taking its own time.

She was in her senior year at Penn and had gone to hear Mr. Z's talk. Gabriella was on midsemester break from Cheyney State College and was spending a few nights in Cynthia's campus apartment and had arrived early for the lecture and saved seats, second row center. Cynthia had a clear view to the stage when she pushed toward her seat. She glanced up and saw Mr. Z's eyes trained on her. She looked right and left to make sure that she was the one garnering his attention. She was. He confirmed it by tilting his head and smiling; his lips curved like a crescent moon in the daytime. The moon shouldn't be visible when it was light out, but there it was, an unexpected pleasure smiling at her.

And now she was seeing the accretion of that smile when he'd shown up in her tiny dorm room in the campus apartment she shared with two other roommates. She was expecting her boyfriend, Macon, the one who lived on her grandmother's block and played love songs on his flute whenever she walked by. Macon had been her steady Eddie safety valve, a reliably tender, present, attentive dream of a boyfriend. But the day before Mr. Z's lecture Macon had asked for an understanding, which Cynthia knew meant that he wanted to see other people. So she was trying to be sexy for Macon when Mr. Z showed up.

She focused on the conglomeration of options to wear to Tish's house, tops and pants and dresses piled on her bed. She whittled down her wardrobe selections to black: palazzo pants, hi-lo top, ballerina flats, crystal necklace, beaded bracelet, drop earrings, pleated clutch purse. She filled in her brows with black pencil and even used black liner under her eyes though she knew that would amplify the severity of her eyes.

She stepped out into the early evening air where a rising moon made foreplay with a purple sky. There was green all around her from the broad-leafed trees. Dusk birds flirted with high notes. Gnats circled. A weeping Japanese maple, elegant with its bounty of wine-colored feathery leaves, almost hid its branches that twisted and gyrated as if seeking relief from some extreme discomfort. Cynthia pulled her phone from her clutch purse and texted Gabriella. *I apparently said his name out loud when I was in the hospital. E and Melanie asked who he was.*

She hit send. She knew that Gabriella would know who she was talking about. She sighed into the twilight air and her breath scattered the gnats, and Tish's house came into view.

Six

Tish looked out the window as she folded teal-and-coral-colored linen napkins at her center-island counter. She was watching for Bloc, though she told herself she was not. That would be new for her, watching for a man. They watched for her. But here she was, eyes locked on the redbrick path that led to her house, watching for Bloc, and seeing Cynthia approach. She was experiencing déjà vu now because the same thing happened yesterday as she'd watched the glass doors to the reception open and close. She'd felt somewhat luxurious yesterday in her silky outfit loaded with tiger stripes, even though the Gen's brunch receptions were more casually attired affairs. She'd smiled and nodded as the regulars arrived, white folk she could get down with: a former hippie who bragged about seeing Jimi up close at Woodstock; an activist who'd put his life on the line registering Black people to vote during Freedom Summer; a feminist who'd burned bras with the other white girls in Atlantic City. However, there were also more than a few closet Trumpers who gave themselves away after the second glass of wine. And then she'd seen Cynthia walk toward the reception room's glass doors. She was excited that another

Black woman had finally moved to the Gen; she was also relieved that Cynthia would not topple her reign as the prettiest tree in theses woods. She knew the latter was a cringeworthy sentiment, but Tish had always been the prettiest one.

Tish was raised in Lawrenceville, a ritzy part of central New Jersey where presentation mattered. Looks mattered. Her mother was a status-conscious social climber who'd nudge Tish to be friends with the other girls who were special like she was special.

What makes them so special, or me? Tish would challenge her mother, defiant tone and posture with her hand on her hip causing her father to suppress his laughter as he nodded and winked because Tish and her father were like-minded. She'd beg her father to rescue her from yet another tea party and take her to Philadelphia so that she could spend weekends with her cousins GG, short for Gordenia, and Willow, the two daughters of her father's sister. They lived on a tidy block in South Philly that always seemed to smell of buttered yeast rolls hot from the oven. She'd grown up thinking that's how heaven must smell. Tish's cousins taught her how to jump double Dutch, how to roller-skate up and down the close blocks, how to play Last Tag with the other children until the streetlights came on; then they'd retire to the front steps and eat water ice and play clapping games and tell stories. They even taught Tish how to code-switch before Tish even knew there was a term for what they did when they'd pepper their language with slang and mismatched subject-verb sentence construction, then when they were someplace like Wanamaker's or the Philadelphia Museum of Art, they'd seamlessly switch to the dialect of the white girls who went to private school.

Tish's aunt doted on her and gave her most of what she asked for, to her cousins' delight. The only request her aunt consistently denied was when Tish would beg her to press her hair as she'd watch her aunt take the comb from the stove, smoke still rising, and pull it through the cousins' hair until their lively coils yielded to a limp straightness. Even though Tish loved GG's and Willow's natural hair that was thick and frothy and felt like her mother's Persian lamb coat, she also had an affinity for the all's right with the world feeling that would take over the smoky breakfast room on Saturday mornings that smelled of Dixie Peach and fried hair. One morning her aunt missed GG's hairline and burned the tip of her ear. Tish cried so hysterically that her aunt had to stop and console Tish as if she were the one who'd been burned. Even GG, rubbing an ice cube over the hot skin, reassured Tish that she was okay, because she was used to it after all.

"Plus she wants to look pretty," her aunt said.

"But she's already pretty," Tish insisted, begging her aunt to stop with the hot comb lest she burn GG again.

Tish once intentionally burned the tip of her own ear. She wanted to be in solidarity with her cousins, wanted to show off her ear scabs to assure GG and Willow that she was no prettier than they were. And Tish's cousins were the prettiest to her anyhow. They were her comrades like her father was. Back then she ascribed to her father's philosophy; he would insist to Tish that she was beautiful for sure, but so was every other little girl. True beauty came from the heart, he'd say; a person's kindness and good works were the real display of beauty.

What did he know? He'd been found dead at a Down-the-Way Philly whorehouse when Tish was eighteen. Tish's demoralized mother changed her name and relocated south to family property in Virginia. Tish took on her mother's new last name and ran away from New Jersey to Southern California for college where no one would know. She remained on the West Coast after undergrad to earn successive master's degrees, one in education, the other in theology, though she had no desire to teach or preach. She worked instead as an administrator for LA County by day, socialite by night, where she cloaked her grief and shame under a rapturous smile, and haute couture fashion, and the pretty-boy men she dangled from her arm like Gucci purses. She managed to erase the idea of her father by doing the opposite of what he'd tried to impart. She'd charm-school-walk into a room and gobble the attention her presence commanded. She used her energy to respond to how people reacted to her prettiness so she didn't have to sink into her interior world where she felt Medusa-ugly. In that way she considered her looks a form of grace that kept her lifted up.

Lately, though, she sensed the grace of her prettiness thinning like her hair was thinning. Though she felt as desirable as she always had, in recent years when she looked in a man's eyes his pupils didn't expand to saucers; he didn't stumble around for words as if the sight of her had made his brain go to mush; if a younger woman crossed his path, Tish would sense his attention pull away from her altogether. So she left LA with its hyperfocus on being young, gifted, and beautiful, but you better be young. She relocated to Philadelphia to be closer to her cousins who now had grandchildren whom she adored. And then two years ago she moved to the Gen to be with the over-fifty-five set to reclaim her grace, to turn heads and drop jaws again, to focus on people focusing on her because that had always been her defense mechanism when difficult emotions surfaced. She felt like a rose in full bloom here, velvety petals and all. But Bloc declining her overtures the other night crystallized what she didn't want to accept: the molecules rising from her essence and floating through the air making her irresistible had lost their mojo. She had become an older woman, and even among her peers, she was no longer the most desirable.

Tish reasoned that's why she'd insulted Bloc so harshly at the reception yesterday. She had actually gone to the reception prepared to make up with Bloc for the way she'd ousted him from her house the other night. But then she noticed him look at Cynthia a beat longer than necessary and she felt her throne tilt, felt herself falling. Even caught herself thinking about her father again. Suddenly she was remembering how she'd tease him for trying to be hip walking around with an Afro pick in the back pocket of his jeans. His eyes would crinkle the way they did when he smiled deeply and he'd break out into Tower of Power's rendition of "What Is Hip?" that would have Tish laughing hysterically. She'd feel herself missing him when that recollection surfaced. She'd will the bitterness to return. The bitterness was easier to manage because it was merely resentment that had hardened, no complexity of textures to plow through, just a solid rock that sat there and let her be.

. . .

Cynthia was on a roller coaster from the time she stepped into Tish's cottage and Tish greeted her effusively with how glad she was that she could make it. Tish had an alto voice that took over the room the way her presence did, too, with her locks wrapped high, adding to her tallness, and her oversized eyes and pert nose and thin lips that still managed to be shaped like a heart. Her lips were colored in a coral tone that complemented the teal-and-coral knife-pleated off-the-shoulder top she wore, and the seamed ankle-length pants, and the chairs and pillows and circle rug; even the artwork hanging was awash in beachscape colors so that the expanse of the room was like an ocean, and Tish like a sea nymph, smiling, gliding. Cynthia prepared herself to ride out the waves, feeling weighty and uninspired in her all black.

Shortly Lavia arrived with bags of takeout from the Peruvian chicken place, apologizing for being late but explaining that Antwon, the Gen's concierge, hadn't arranged for the pickup and delivery she'd scheduled, and how unlike him that was.

"I hope he's okay," Lavia said, as she pushed her off-centered bang away from her forehead.

"Why wouldn't he be okay?" Tish asked.

"Because, he always does what he says he's going to do,

always. Not letting me know that he couldn't make it is so out of character for him."

"That is very unlike him," Tish agreed, as she explained to Cynthia that Antwon was akin to their adopted nephew. "He was part of a mentoring program sponsored by the homeowners association, and Bloc found out that he was unhoused, so we got the management company to hire him as a live-in concierge with a nice benefits package that includes tuition reimbursement, so he's now in school working towards a degree in the hospitality industry."

"Well that's good to know the association is socially conscious," Cynthia said.

"And speaking of being social, Cynthia," Lavia said, "I hope Tish hasn't been on her typically bad behavior."

"Oh no, she's making me feel right at home," Cynthia said.

"Ooh, should I feel sorry for the state of your home, then," Lavia quipped.

Cynthia laughed then, and Tish said that she thought she and Lavia were sisters in another lifetime.

"Lavia shows me no love; my cousins who are siblings are the same way with one another," Tish said, as she uncorked wine.

The doorbell chimed and Lavia giggled. "That must be Bloc, speaking of showing no love."

"Girl, you better hush," Tish said, as she picked up her phone to unlock the door. "I feel really bad about insulting him at that reception, so, please, let's not revisit that tonight."

"Okay, *sister*," Lavia said, teasingly, as she winked at Cynthia and Tish began pouring the wine and Bloc walked in.

Bloc was in another gingham shirt, this one navy and white, and Cynthia wondered what was it with him in the gingham; was it serendipitous, or did he know somehow that the orderly sequence of those tiny squares affected her? She took a long sip of wine to hide the fact that she was blushing. She had never been the blushing type, but she felt sixteen again, or maybe sixteen for the first time because with the mother she'd had, she'd never gotten the chance to know what sixteen was like.

Tish looked Bloc up and down and smiled a flirty smile, the way Cynthia wanted to but she'd never been that bold. "Well, well, well, and what to my wandering eyes should appear," Tish said.

"But a miniature sled and eight tiny reindeer." Lavia finished the line of the poem, then said, "Yeah yeah, I know 'The Night Before Christmas,' too."

"Well, I hope that doesn't make me Santa Claus?" Bloc joked. "That's a lot of pressure."

"Oh, I've got the sense you're up to the task," Tish said.

"Miniature sled and all," Lavia said, and Tish furrowed her brow at her.

"And you remember Cynthia from the reception yesterday, right?" Tish said then.

"Yes, of course I remember Cynthia from the reception," he said. "Nice to see you again, Cynthia."

That's all he said. Said it as if he'd last seen her at Wegmans and had not just spent the past day and night on her air mattress.

"Nice to see you as well," Cynthia replied, conceding to herself that she had no idea how to otherwise respond except to

79

drink more wine to try and douse the fireball of emotions growing in her stomach.

The dancing helped. At Lavia's insistence Tish changed the music from Bill Withers to James Brown hollering about breaking out in a cold sweat. Lavia flailed her arms and danced to the middle of the great room. "I love James Brown. Come on, dance with me, Cynthia."

"You're free to ignore her," Tish said, refilling Cynthia's wineglass.

"Who can resist 'Cold Sweat,' though," Cynthia said, as she took cha-cha steps toward Lavia and Lavia grabbed her hands and they spun each other around. The music streamed into Earth, Wind & Fire's "Mighty Mighty," and Tish started singing about being people of the sun, and then belted out the line about the truth you can't run from. She moved her slim hips easily from side to side, leaned in with her shoulders, and snapped her fingers to the beat. "Ah, ah, ah," she sang, holding the notes, as she turned her back on Bloc and put her hands on her knees and bounced her butt.

"Oh my god," Lavia shrieked. "Look at Tish, she's doing that . . . that . . . what do you call that, Cynthia?"

"Twerking," Cynthia said, as she eased away from what had become the dance floor. Cynthia knew how to twerk, too, thought about showing them how it was really done since she had hips. But she took a seat at the center-island counter, reminding herself that in her entire life she'd never gotten into a competition with another woman over a man. She had no intentions of starting at this stage in her life.

When the dancing was done, Tish walked around and re-filled the wineglasses, Lavia began uncovering the trays, and Bloc took a seat across from Cynthia and pulled out his leather satchel that Cynthia knew held his pipe and his weed.

"And may I ask what you think you're doing?" Tish pointed to the satchel. "Just because you're a pothead does not mean everybody is. Can you at least ask Cynthia if she minds if you smoke around her? Contact highs are a real thing, you know."

"My apologies," Bloc said, as he bowed in Cynthia's direction. "Do you partake of the devil's weed?"

"That depends on who the devil is," Cynthia said. Though she wanted to say more. Wanted to say, *What do you think? Didn't I just suck on your pipe yesterday before I took you out of your hard-on misery.*

"Hmm, who is the devil," Bloc said, chuckling. "Let's just say I know a guy, so it's all good."

"Look out, Cynthia," Lavia said, "when someone says it's all good, it's usually mostly all bad. But if it puts you at ease, I'll go first."

Bloc lit the pipe and Lavia drew in hard, then coughed. "Damn, that's potent," she said, as she leaned back on the counter stool and swiveled it around in half circles.

Tish waved her hands motioning Bloc. "Let me see what you bringing. I hope it's better than that weak shit you brought in here last week."

"Uh, I assume you're referring to the weed, Tish," Lavia said. Tish shot Lavia a look, and Lavia laughed and said, "Ignore me, please, I did not just say that."

"Uh-oh, Bloc," Tish said, coughing and exhaling smoke as she did, "you brought the killer with you tonight, huh, baby."

"I bring the killer with me every time, Miss Lady," Bloc said, as he walked to the other side of the counter to offer Cynthia the pipe. "You just got to know what to do with it."

"Whoa," Lavia said, as her eyes shot way open. "I'm feeling like this is a conversation between a and b, and right now my name is c."

"Right?" Cynthia said, as she nodded in agreement and took the pipe. "So do I just, you know, inhale? It's been a while." She talked more to the pipe than to Bloc as she tried to keep the edge from her voice. Tried to keep the fireball in her stomach manageable by doing what she'd learned in therapy and give a name to what she was feeling to shrink the emotion. She thought it was all anger: at Bloc for spouting that bullshit before he disappeared into the mist this morning about not wanting the dream to end; at Tish and her self-assured silly dance moves; at her son for trying to micromanage her life; at whoever the Quick Draw McGraw type was who'd made the offer on her house so immediately; at her double-wide staircase that had betrayed her like her then husband had; at the black funeral outfit she was wearing that was making her back itch; at herself, mostly angry at herself, she felt like such a fool; and now a seed was stuck in the damn pipe so that she couldn't even get a decent hit.

"It's not working," she said, as she snatched the pipe from her mouth and handed it to Bloc.

"Not working—"

"Something's stuck, I can't get anything."

"How long has it been since you last smoked?" Tish asked, as Bloc tore off a piece of foil and dumped the contents of the pipe and swept away several seeds clumped together.

"I don't even remember the last time—"

"Really? I thought everyone had a last-got-high story; you know, like knowing exactly where you were when Kennedy was assassinated."

"Well, I can tell you when Kennedy was shot I was at Hamilton Elementary School sitting at a wooden desk; you know, the kind of desk where the seat was connected, and the principal called a special assembly and I cried nonstop for hours. That I remember. I guess the circumstances that surrounded my last high were just pathetically uneventful because it's a total blank."

She sensed Bloc stiffen when she said that as he restuffed the pipe and offered it to her. "Well, let's see if we can make this get-high memorable," he said. "Do you need for me to explain what you should do?"

"I can figure it out," she said, as she took the pipe, managing not to snatch it, and drew in hard and held the smoke deep in her stomach. She felt the immediate rush of the pings shooting through her head, felt her anger begin to thin, rippling in and out in waves as Lavia asked if she and Bloc knew each other from when they lived in Western Philadelphia.

"West," Bloc and Cynthia said simultaneously, correcting her.

"Okay then, west, West Philadelphia," Lavia said. "My goodness, people from Philadelphia are the most neighborhood-centric people I know."

"You must have never met anyone from Brooklyn, then,"

Tish said, as she poured more wine and raised her glass toasting Cynthia's move to the Gen. "To Cynthia," they all repeated.

Cynthia thanked them for welcoming her so generously and looked directly at Bloc, the first time she had all evening. She saw that pained expression that had covered his face when he'd talked about his ex-wife the day before. She wondered if he was feeling remorse for treating her as if yesterday hadn't happened. She restrained herself from feeling sorry for him right now, thinking how drunk she must be to take pity on him. But holding on to her anger was exhausting.

Lavia stood and pulled her phone from her pants pocket, prompting Tish to say, "Lavia must think she's still twenty the way she walks around with her phone in her pants pocket."

"Well, I couldn't wear my phone in my pants pocket if I wanted to, my pants are to capacity with my pockets empty." Cynthia, emboldened from all the wine, said it for Bloc's ears, though she smiled in Tish's direction.

"Aw, girl, you look good," Tish said, as she picked up her wineglass and raised it and nodded at Cynthia. Cynthia was struck by her sincerity.

"She does look good," Bloc said. "You all do. I'm just an ugly weed among beautiful velvety roses."

"Good? Did you say someone looks good?" Tish said, as she flung her hands dramatically and showed off her teal-colored gelled nails. Then, as if she were on a runway at Fashion Week, she strode from behind the island and did a catwalk through the great room. She twirled in the middle of her great room that was decorated in colors of the ocean and sky and sand, she herself looking like a glorious sunset in the middle of it all, as if she were saying *I know I'm in my sixties and on the descent here; I know the night is coming, but I still got some sky to travel, and this ball of fire is not going down without one more grand display.*

Cynthia admired Tish's ability to do that. She thought about her own inevitable sunset. How would she yield to the night? *Carefully,* she thought, *too damn carefully,* as Tish told everyone to help themselves to Lavia's food offerings, and they heaped their plates with chicken and rice and beans, the munchies having already set in. Then Lavia blurted, "See, I knew all was not well with Antwon," as she stared at her phone.

"What happened to my young boy?" Bloc asked, as he poured sauce over his chicken and ate a forkful.

"Apparently he was pulled over by the police for a broken taillight."

Bloc put down his fork. "This can't end well; please don't tell me they tased him."

"No, but they did arrest him for an outstanding summary offense."

"What?" Bloc said. "For a got damned summary offense?"

"What's a summary offense anyhow?" Tish asked.

"Such a minor infraction that it doesn't even rise to the level of a misdemeanor," Bloc said, his voice husky with emotion. "Essentially, it's when the cops want to eff with you and can't conjure up a crime to pin on you; this shit pisses me off so damn much, shit like this doesn't happen to the white boys."

Tish squeezed the back of Bloc's neck. "Right?"

"I love that kid. Reminds me of me at that age," Bloc said, as he poured himself more wine.

"Excuse me, Bloc," Lavia said, "didn't you go to the Ivy League? Antwon's at a community college."

"And that matters why?"

"Because you were in a privileged education setting—"

"Doesn't change a thing about being a young Black man in America. I've yet to see a cop ask for a matric card; hell, that might make matters worse 'cause then they'll call you uppity and make it their personal responsibility to bring you back down to where they think you should be, spread-eagle on the ground. When did this happen? Are they still holding him? I can put up money to bail him out."

"Roy's already on it," Lavia said. "He sent an email—"

"Roy," Bloc said, pausing to swallow. "Why the eff is that racist Roy involved?"

"Well, he was a judge," Tish offered. "And Maze was a public defender, makes sense. They know people, they can be helpful. And I wouldn't call him a racist. Maybe a tad unevolved."

"Bloc, you're still holding a grudge against Roy because he mistook you for the porter?" Lavia said, then turned to Cynthia and asked her if she'd heard that story.

Cynthia nodded. "Tish told me, happened a couple of years ago, right?" She directed her words at Lavia.

"Exactly," Lavia said. "Two years is a long time."

"Not long enough to erase the insult of it in my mind. Mo eff-er might as well have called me boy. Y'all forgive me for getting worked up, but this bullshit with Antwon goes right to my core."

"I know it does," Tish said. "That shit is triggering for me, too."

"Triggering for you, Tish?" Lavia asked, as she scrolled through her phone. "Aren't you a child of the light-complexion Black elite? Don't you all play by different rules?"

"Excuse me, Lavia, but that whole complexion thing is just a ploy to divide and conquer Black people. Furthermore, what you do not understand, as Stevie sings, is that you can't cash in your face. I don't care about the degree of eliteness you walking around with. A Black person in America is still a Black person in America."

"Preach, sister," Cynthia said, as she drained her wine, and already Tish was pouring more. "You ain't said nothing but a word. And I for one would never want to cash in my face. For all my struggles as a Black woman, I would never want to be anything but a Black woman."

"And all the Black men are very happy about that," Bloc said, as Cynthia dusted nonexistent crumbs from her top so she didn't have to look at Bloc to see if he was looking at her.

"I really hate to interrupt this Black Panther rally," Lavia said, "but I've received another note from Roy indicating that Antwon's situation is more complex than originally thought. Details are sketchy, he says, but he'll be back in touch with info and a request for donations once he's established a defense fund."

"A defense fund? That's serious. Sounds like someone's trying to set up my young boy," Bloc said. "Probably trying to pin some old shit on him. Or worse, somebody else's old shit."

"And we all carrying around old shit, right?" Tish said. "I don't care how squeaky clean we purport to be, we've all broken the law, from burning through a red light, to stretching the truth on our tax returns, to killing."

"Ah, you lost me at killing," Lavia said.

"Not like literally killing a person," Tish went on. "But we all have caused the death of maybe somebody's dream, or murdered a relationship, or choked the air out of a person's joy, or drowned someone's optimism. Even if it wasn't our intention to do so. You know what I mean, don't you, Cynthia?"

Cynthia felt a rush of silence swirl through the room as all attention turned to her. She swallowed the wine left in her glass and shook her head back and forth and looked at Tish sitting across the counter glistening in her teal and coral like Glinda the good witch. She reminded her of Gabriella right now.

"Well, yes, even if it wasn't our intention," Cynthia said, as her tongue grew increasingly heavy in her mouth and she felt her words slurring. "I'm really, really sorry for it too. And it wasn't entirely my fault. But you know, I helped it along. And right now I feel really bad about that, really bad. And I'm also very high and a little drunk, or very drunk and a little high, not sure which right now. And I'm rambling, but I've got so many feelings." Her eyes welled up and she just let them spill over.

"Aw, I hear you, girl," Tish said, as she went to Cynthia and put her arm around Cynthia's shoulder and pulled her in a hug. "But whatever it is, you've got to forgive yourself."

"Thank you, Tish. I like you," Cynthia said.

"I like you, too, baby," Tish said, as she half walked, half stumbled back to sit down. "And if you want to talk about it, just know you're among friends. We let it all hang out here. Don't we, guys?"

"No holds barred," Bloc said, as he raised his glass in Cynthia's direction. She dried her eyes and swallowed more wine as they affirmed Bloc's no-holds-barred proclamation and began trading stories about their pasts.

Bloc told of throwing a brick through the window of a furniture store on Ridge Avenue the night Martin Luther King was assassinated. Tish sobbed into her teal-colored napkin that matched her nail polish and eyeshadow as she talked about the abortion she'd arranged for her cousin when they were sixteen; thank god all went as planned, but the sound of her cousin crying out in pain still haunted her. Lavia said she used to be a sex worker and ended up killing her john. They all looked at her stunned, and she said, "Sike, you guys are too easy." They managed to laugh then.

Even Cynthia chuckled as she tried not to succumb to the "I trust you, you can trust me" vibe that was coming for her as the weed high bounced in her head like helium balloons drifting toward heaven and the wine went down softly, easily. The playlist had mellowed into John Coltrane; his saxophone on "In a Sentimental Mood" was churning her insides to butter. Even the night got in on the act with its silky appearance pouncing through the skylights. In the brief while she'd lived here, Cynthia preferred the nights. With all the windowed walls and ceilings in theses cottages, the daylight had free rein to push itself in and flop like an uninvited guest pretending to care, but really just trying to fish through her past. The night came with no pretense. She could trust the night.

She poured water into her glass from the crystal pitcher floating limes. She gulped the water. She hadn't realized how thirsty she was, for the water, for this: What was this gathering, anyhow, a kind of drinking-of-the-wine communion where they testified to what the Lord had brought them through the way they did at her grandmother's church? She'd hated going to church as a child in her patent leather shoes and newly pressed hair and eyelet cotton dress that topped an itchy crinoline slip. Until she got inside and nestled next to Rose, who smelled of Jean Naté cologne and spearmint gum. She'd feel a stirring that she feared might be the prelude to the uncontrollable shouting and flailing and dancing of the holy women. She thought she'd rather die than make such a spectacle of herself, so she'd suppress the stirring and pretend to be bored and tug Rose's arm and ask her if they could leave yet. Even though she truly wanted to stay and listen and hear and feel. And testify.

Cynthia refilled her water tinged with lime and started testifying now. She told them how when she was a student she tried to shoplift a textbook from Penn's bookstore. "It was a big-ass book, *Shakespeare's Complete Works*, and expensive as hell so I guess my trying to steal the book was a revolutionary act, or so I told myself. My boyfriend was with me and I helped him get the book into the inside pocket of his oversized army coat. It was kind of thrilling 'cause I was that good girl who followed all the rules. We were almost to the exit when this security guard flagged us."

"White or Black?" Bloc asked.

"Does it matter?" Lavia asked.

"Black," Cynthia said.

"Uncle ass Tom," Bloc said.

"Then this big white one joined him—"

"That's what they do—" Bloc interrupted. "The white boy probably wanted to make the first move but sent the brother to deflect accusations of being racist—"

"Well, they *were* stealing, weren't they?" Lavia asked.

"Can Cynthia finish her story, please?" Tish said.

"Anyhow, they jostled him through the bookstore to this back room, all the white people looking at him like yeah, that's what they all do. And I didn't do anything, you know; I didn't say anything to defend him. I didn't say that it was my idea, that the book was for my class, that I was the one who put the book in his coat, you know; I just let him take the fall. That was so fucked-up of me." She fought tears again. "And he was such a good guy."

"I bet he was fine, too," Tish said, as she refilled Cynthia's water glass. "I only say that because you've got hips and the girls with hips always landed the fine dudes."

"Is that true?" Lavia asked.

"Not hardly true," Cynthia said. "Where I'm from all the guys were trying to stand a chance with the tall, slim beauties like you, Tish." She raised her glass in Tish's direction.

"They were superficial posers, though," Tish said, as she reached across the counter to clink Cynthia's glass. "I liked the bad boys. Somebody willing to steal a textbook for me would have had my heart."

"Did they actually arrest him?" Bloc asked. "For a damn textbook?"

"They did not. He said they tried to scare him with the threat of prosecution. But he knew enough to know the price of the book barely rose to petty larceny."

"Did y'all stay together after that?" Tish asked.

"We did, for a while. I'm not lying when I say he was a good person through and through."

"Is that who you were talking about when you cried just a bit ago?" Tish asked, almost whispering.

"It is," Cynthia lied. "I guess that was the beginning of killing what we had between us." She had to lie. She was really thinking about Mr. Z. No amount of trust, wine or weed, hypnosis, meditation, laying on of hands, chanting, juju, yoga, psychotherapy, mushrooms, or the holy dance could loosen her enough to talk about him to anyone except Gabriella.

Lavia's voice pulled Cynthia back to the great room that, with its oversupply of coral and teal, felt like a sunset over a Caribbean sea. "I finally found the original email again from Roy. Okay. I know it's going to go *Twilight Zone* on me and disappear again, so before Rod Serling jumps on my screen, do you guys want to hear it?"

"You know what," Bloc said, "excuse me for using the f-word in mixed company, but fuck Roy. I'm going to the county jail myself first thing in the morning and see what's going on."

"And personally, Lavia, I'd rather see Rod Serling on your screen," Cynthia said.

"*The Twilight Zone* was the bomb, wasn't it?" Tish said, and she and Cynthia slapped hands. "'Submitted for your approval.'" She imitated Rod Serling's voice as Cynthia both sniffed and laughed.

"I think Hitchcock was spookier. *The Birds* scared the living crap out of me. For months after that movie, I would run if I saw more than two pigeons in the sky at the same time. But hey, I could go for some Rod Serling," Bloc said, putting more chicken and rice on his plate. "In fact, I got a few *Twilight Zone* stories of my own."

Lavia stood and pushed her phone back in her pocket. "Well, Bloc, you got to get another bowl working just for me if this is transitioning into story hour. I was ready to dance. You all tired, old-acting people are surely going to put me to sleep."

"Sleep on, sister girl," Tish said, as she went into the great room and sank into the paisley armchair and put her feet up on the ottoman. "All of you are welcome. Just as long as you are outta here by ten in the morning, 'cause my cousin is coming with her granddaughter, who is like my granddaughter. I don't want to have to do no 'splaining about who these hungover people are sprawled all over my great room."

"That would be funny," Cynthia said, as she refilled her wineglass and curled up on the corner of the couch. My son almost caught me yesterday afternoon—" She stopped herself and sipped her wine.

"What happened yesterday afternoon?" Tish asked, sitting up.

"Mmm, girl, that's another story for another time," Cynthia said. "I'd much rather hear Bloc spook us with his *Twilight Zone* tale."

"Actually, I'd rather hear you." Tish moved the ottoman and leaned forward. "Come on, don't hold back. Sounds like your story got some juice to it. What your son almost catch you doing?"

"No biggie, really," Cynthia said, looking at Bloc's face now as he walked toward the couch holding his plate. Now he was the one avoiding eye contact.

"I think you holding out," Tish said, as she leaned back and replaced her feet on the ottoman. "What you think, Bloc, you think Cynthia's holding out on us?"

"She said, no biggie, guess that means no biggie," Bloc said, as he sat in the straight-backed armless chair. "All right, as soon I wolf down this chicken, I'm ready to tell my *Twilight Zone* tale. Who wants to hear it?"

"Can I be the first to yell out, 'not me.'" Lavia groaned as she stretched out on the rug.

"Once upon a time there was a kid named Blankwood," Bloc began.

"Oh Lord," Lavia said. "Cynthia, in case you don't know, that's Bloc's given name. They must have been confused at his birth 'cause they gave him a last name for a first name, and a first name for a last. His last name is Bob."

"Damn. Mr. Blankwood Bob," Cynthia said to their laughter. "It's all good, all good indeed. Mr. Blankwood Bob."

Seven

They slept through Bloc's story: Lavia on her back on the rug; Cynthia curled up in a fetal position on the couch; Tish sunk into the wide-backed, wide-armed corner chair with her legs propped on the ottoman. He'd thought it was a good story, absent all references to Mr. Rochester, or that beautiful lab, Shelly, or the fact that he'd been known as Blockhead as a child. In the farce he'd just told, a boy named Blankwood foiled a thug who'd waved around a switchblade as he'd tried to rob Scotty's store while his mother worked behind the counter. Blankwood came to own the switchblade after he kicked the blade from the robber's hand and he and Scotty wrestled the man to the floor. In the *Twilight Zone*-ish twist on the story, the switchblade never punctured the skin of a good person, no matter how hard its sharpness was drawn against the flesh. But a person with evil intentions would hemorrhage from just a tap of the blade.

Had they not all been asleep, Bloc would have pulled out his own switchblade as a grand finale, the one Scotty had gifted him the day Bloc realized he wasn't slow. He still used the switchblade.

But they were all asleep and Bloc was relieved that they were.

Especially relieved that Cynthia's eyes were closed. Her eyes were so intense. They didn't dance like Tish's eyes that always seemed poised to tease a man to take him down. Tish's gaze had a lightness about it that made it easy for him to defend himself by holding her at a comfortable distance. There was no such defense with Cynthia. There was just her naked stare with a starkness so hot that it threatened to melt the barrier he worked so hard to maintain, and a kindness so severe that it terrified him. She'd been so kind when she'd relieved him of his engorgement the day before. Now he resented her for it. Reasoned that's why he'd acted as if the last time he'd seen her was at the reception yesterday. He knew that his behavior would preempt him being with Cynthia again. He thought that was likely best. Next thing, he'd be babbling to Cynthia like a little boy confessing to all he'd done.

He'd certainly had to look away from Cynthia earlier when he was telling the story about throwing the brick through the storefront window on Ridge Avenue after Martin Luther King's assassination. Her eyes may have shaken the truth out of him. The truth was that the brick he'd thrown wasn't through a storefront window, and it had nothing to do with the riots after Martin Luther King was shot, but everything to do with his third wife.

On Sunday mornings before the stores opened that would feed Coral's shopping addiction, Coral would push into the guts of North Philly, or even all the way to the most decimated parts of Chester to the holiness churches that boasted some of the broadest-backed men she'd ever known.

Bloc had followed her one morning to the nether reaches of Chester and watched her park her car on an alley-sized street and then make her way to the corner and into the storefront of the All Saints Deliverance Tabernacle. He could hear the tambourines and drums even through the thick glass of his Lincoln XL. He realized that this was her secret, that she found her God in churches like this. He started to cry from relief, and from guilt, too, that he had suspected something darker. But then he saw her come back out, her hair with the copper-toned highlights frizzed up from the heat of the place. She moved quickly down the alley block where she'd parked her car. As he waited to hear her drive away, he saw a man leave the church and look both ways as if the desolate corner were a four-lane highway. He was in a shiny suit; the pinstripes were irregularly spaced and missed each other at the shoulder. He walked past a construction site toward the alley street and looked around again and turned in to it. Bloc waited a minute and got out of his car and took the same path the man in the garish suit had. He stepped over empty baggies and Burger King boxes and blades of new grass and he'd had the thought of what a good sermon topic the new grass would make: no matter the place or the circumstance or the depravity of the soul, God always allows the grass to grow.

There was his wife's car. The windows were already fogged and it seemed that the church service had moved inside the car, too, the way that it shook. He ran back to his own car. He thought he could hear them inside the church singing run, run, running for Jesus. He ran faster still, managing to outpace the music. But he could still hear the music as he sat in his car with the windows up. He could hear it long after the church had emptied, even after night fell and softened the desolation of the corner. He eased out of his car then. He picked up a brick from the construction site and hurled it toward the church window to try and make the music stop. The stained glass was old and solid and didn't yield to the brick. He stood there and sobbed then. He'd wanted to throw a brick through Rochester's window. But he never got the chance.

Eight

A month into Cynthia's life at the Gen, and Bloc had yet to re-visit her carriage house, nor did she venture over to his. They encountered each other at the herbarium where she went to buy her essential oils; or when they were seated at the same table on the evenings when she took her dinner in the crystal dining hall that tried to replicate Wanamaker's Crystal Tea Room. She'd joined him and a dozen other residents when they'd gone to the county courthouse in a show of support for Antwon at his bail hearing. She'd smoke Bloc's weed and laugh at his jokes on the nights when she'd pull on some tight pants and strappy sandals and a blouson-type off-the-shoulder top that hid the pout at the bottom of her stomach and step over to Tish's. She'd mostly convinced herself that she was not offended by the way he'd erased their day and night together out of existence. Sometimes she told herself that maybe he was in the early stages of Alzheimer's and his recent memories couldn't even be recorded over the excessive protein deposits mummifying his brain. Other times she'd wonder if his behavior was normal for people their age, the way it was normal for people to hook up at a disco in 1977 to the sounds of Donna Summer singing "Love to Love You Baby." She'd even had the thought that their time on her air mattress had been more than just sex for him, much more than her relieving him of his misery; hadn't he acknowledged as much when he'd left that morning after? He'd kissed her mouth in back-and-forth slow brushes and said that he hoped he hadn't dreamt their time together. Maybe he'd convinced himself it was a dream. Then there were the times when she'd challenge herself to confront him, spurred on by Gabriella when they managed lengthy, fractured phone conversations over the life-affirming sounds of Gabriella's triplet grandchildren squealing and howling and playing, fighting, falling, crying in the background. Gabriella insisted more than once that Cynthia should call the song exactly what it was, stressing that Cynthia shouldn't avoid direct contact with Bloc. "I mean, y'all slept together. I would act like it. Make him as uncomfortable as you are. Your hiding in full view of him is letting him off too easy. Who does that anyhow? Has sex with someone and then acts as if it never happened. Motherfucker," Gabriella said, and then gasped, and said to the triplets, "You did not just hear Grandmom say that word," over a chorus of the triplets clamoring, "Motherfucker? Motherfucker? What's a motherfucker? Whose mommy is named fucker, Grandmom?"

Cynthia laughed so hard until she made snorting sounds. "I have to facetime with the triplets when you have them next and thank them, 'cause I don't remember when I've laughed so fully. But in the meantime, please text me more pictures of those cuties, please," Cynthia said.

"Just remember you asked," Gabriella said, and Cynthia could hear the gushing in her voice. "And Speaking of texting pictures, can you text me some more pictures of your peeps?"

"Why," Cynthia giggled, "does Bloc look like an axe murderer in the last one I sent?"

"Not Bloc, necessarily. Something about your girl Tish, though."

"Tish? What about Tish?"

"I'm not sure yet, but I think I've seen her before."

"Really? Where? I mean, she's from Virginia and California, but she does have Philly cousins."

"And what's her last name?"

"Jones, why, do you know her?"

"I don't think I've actually met her, but you know me and my gift for remembering faces from eons ago. Just send me more pics so I can figure it out."

Cynthia said that she would. She was able to swat away the creeping anxiety over what Gabriella might be looking for. She'd gotten better at shrinking her anxious thoughts of late.

It helped that Cynthia had been taking full advantage of the Sexagenarian's wellness services to get at least some of her money's worth from the astronomical association fees. She regularly did downward-facing dog and the plow and cobra poses at the chichi yoga studio where the walls were lavender, the floors were teak, and the mats smelled of vanilla and mint. She'd swum in all three of the pools and had taken water aerobics classes, Zumba classes, a throwback Jazzercise-type class. She'd closed her eyes and inhaled and exhaled long, slow breaths and relaxed her mind as instructed by the mindfulness coach as she perched on a vinyl cushion next to the creek that smelled of lilies and baked earth. She felt looser, lighter, thinner as a result.

The one thing, though, that all the mindfulness sessions, walks through iris-lined trails, and even conversations with Gabriella had not remedied for Cynthia was her lapses into recollections of Mr. Z. She'd thought about him more in the month that she'd lived at the Gen than she had in the decades since the end of their relationship. She'd wondered if their relationship really ever ended since it felt so immediate, so in her bones when he'd drift into her conscious mind. She'd think that she'd still be in a relationship with him on her dying bed, with no reconciliation.

At the moment, nestled in a booth at the Throwback enjoying a milkshake as "We Are Family" poured from the jukebox, Cynthia was free of thoughts of Mr. Z. She'd just been to the movies with Tish and Lavia. They'd seen *Girls Trip* and were rehashing their favorite scenes, laughing as ferociously now as they had in the theater. Cynthia felt her laughter springing from a place of pure joy. She said as much to Tish and Lavia as she turned her straw around and pulled the shake's thick sweetness into her mouth. "I like it here. And I know you guys are well aware how much I hated this place when I first moved in. But now, I'm, like, well, damn, I'm having a good-ass time."

"Aw," Tish gushed. "I'm happy for you. It's partially me, right? You can admit it. I've made it my personal goal to ease your transition to the Gen. I know how you loved your house and your block and your neighborhood."

"And I hellllped," Lavia said, putting a southern drawl on the word *help*.

"Oh my god, did you just do the little girl from that Shake 'n Bake commercial from back in the day?" Cynthia asked.

"Damn, you nailed it, Lavia," Tish said. "How do you come up with all this obscure shit from years ago, and then go vacuous on us when we reference something obvious having to do with current times?"

Cynthia was curious, too, as they all sat back to accommodate the server spreading the table with their food. Cynthia was facing the front of the restaurant and enjoying the view that included a trio of mammoth variegated spruce trees. She marveled at their enduring splendor; even after being yanked from some other place and hauled here and set down in this strange soil, they'd retained their majesty. Then her view was interrupted by Roy in his blue linen blazer and golf shirt. She said a silent prayer that he please not come into the restaurant. She didn't like Roy. Though she and Maze were budding friends, Cynthia had come to share Bloc's opinion about Roy and his mantle of superiority. She sensed that he looked down on her when they had occasion to interact during the times they'd shared a table in the dining room, or chatted at a Gen-sponsored social event, or waited for Chinese takeout. She couldn't tell if it was because she was Black, or a woman, or the combination, or that she was from West Philly, or that she hadn't gone to law school. She finally decided it didn't matter, he was an asshole, with his detestable air of better-than-ness.

Her prayer wasn't answered as the bell over the door clanged an off-key note announcing his entrance. She guessed she grimaced in that instant because Tish turned around to see who she was looking at and waved him over, because of course she would.

Cynthia said a quick hello and then busied herself pouring catsup over her burger and fries. To Cynthia's irritation, Tish invited Roy to join them. Cynthia pretended not to hear the exchange and made no effort to slide over as she asked Lavia if she could get a forkful of her salad to garnish her burger. Then Tish asked her directly if she could move over a smidgeon so that Roy could scoot in next to her. "Oh sure," Cynthia said. "Just give me a sec to fancy my burger." She took her time spreading the endive over the steaming patty, then centering a mushroom cap atop. She knew she was being passive-aggressive; she should have just said, *Actually, Roy, nothing personal, but this is a girls-out evening.*

Once he settled in, Tish told him that they'd just seen the most hilarious movie.

"I know, *Girls Trip,* I did as well," Roy said. "I saw you all leaving but I couldn't catch up with you."

Cynthia almost choked on her burger as she turned to look at him. He seemed so proud of himself, as if he should receive a special commendation for sitting through a raucous comedy about four Black women, twenty years out of college, harking back to their much wilder selves on a let-it-all-hang-out trip to New Orleans; as if he were now on the same level as a few of the other white men Cynthia had come to know here who were true social justice activists and had the body of work and scars—one had been roughed up on the Edmund Pettus Bridge—to prove it.

"Did you enjoy it?" Lavia asked.

"I found it interesting," he said.

"Hmm," Cynthia said. "Interesting that you found it interesting. Since I don't think that was the film's intent, to be interesting."

"What was its intent?" Roy asked, as he scanned the menu.

"To allow us two hours to forget about how effed up everything is now having to do with politics and the state of the country and the world—"

"And invite us instead to laugh our asses off." Lavia jumped in.

"Although I think that the filmmakers would be complimented that they'd managed to hold the interest of a white guy," Tish said, smiling at Roy.

"I think they're more complimented by the fact that their target audience, Black women, showed up for them. I read that the film smashed box office records," Cynthia said.

"Well, nothing wrong with a little crossover appeal." Tish looked at Roy as she spoke.

"Nothing special about it, either," Cynthia said. "Not in this case when the film was already going to be a hit."

"Well, may I ask you, Cynthia," Roy said, still bent over the menu, and Cynthia felt her stomach tighten, "who did you see yourself as?"

"Excuse me?"

"Well, since you went to Penn in the seventies where parties abounded, which character would have been you in that bar scene?"

"How do you know I went to parties? I could have been that nerd who stayed sequestered in my dorm room."

"So you lived in the dorm?"

"I did."

"Well, forgive my presumptions. Perhaps you were that model student who stayed in the library and went to lectures for your socializing."

"That's closer to me."

"Do you have a favorite lecturer?"

"Excuse me."

"Penn has always been known for attracting the best and brightest to campus. Just wondering if a particular talk stands out in your mind."

"I'd have to give it some thought, Roy," Cynthia said, as she felt her breaths turn shallow. "Forty years for me since undergrad."

And there he was, Mr. Z. Though this time he didn't sneak into her thoughts the way he usually did. Right now she saw his approach the way a hiker would look up and see a panther pouncing from a mountaintop coming for her. She covered her throat as if to protect her jugular. The milkshake felt sour in her stomach. She shifted in the booth as she half listened to Tish and Lavia talk about the lecturers they remembered.

"Still drawing a blank, Cynthia?" Roy asked, as he drummed his fingers on the table.

"You know what, I could give you an exhaustive list as I think about it, but right now this milkshake is doing what milkshakes do to me that I've been in denial about for years. So you guys must excuse me. I'm gonna head in before things get ugly."

"Aw, girl, you okay?" Tish asked.

"I didn't mean to chase you away," Roy said, as he stood so Cynthia could exit.

"Wow, Roy, you really think you've got some superpowers," Lavia said.

"Nope, nope, nope," Cynthia said, as she grabbed her purse and slid from the booth. "My best to Maze. Catch you later, Tish and Lavia."

The short order called to her as she made her way to the door. "My lady, you good? I was just 'bout to hit some 'Hot Fun in the Summertime' on the jukebox just for you."

"Definitely taking a rain check on that," she said as she managed a smile and wave and stepped into the air that smelled like Christmas from the spruce trees. Not one of the merry Christmases, though, but the one where her mother overslept because she'd been up all night with her company, likely someone who should have been at his own house putting together a train set or a bike before his own children woke. The tree smelled dank, spoiled, as if it had stood in the pot too long.

Cynthia crossed the street to the other side of the Shops at the Gen where the tony boutiques each had a different-colored awning: red, orange, yellow, green, blue, indigo, and violet to mimic a rainbow. The shops featured everything from fashionable orthotic footwear, to the newest wonder leaf, or seed, or essential oil, claiming to rejuvenate it all: the brain, the eyes, the heart, the skin, so many products for the skin. She passed the winery, the bookshop, the yoga pants store, the store with organic cotton baby clothes, because of course the grandchildren.

The herbarium and confectionery expelled competing aromas; right now mint and butter toffee predominated. The toffee reminded her of the home she'd just left, the mint of her grandmother's house, the combination she thought defined her. Sharp blasts of wit and wisdom, though hardened the way that toffee was hardened, butter and sugar blended and then put through the heat of living: childhood traumas, calamitous indiscretions of young adulthood; marriage blossomed until the drought when they could either dig in deep for water and the long haul, or say the hell with it and let the union die of thirst; career that rose and rose despite the racism, sexism, then petered because of ageism. Contemporaries began to fall away like dominoes then. And suddenly life was finite after all, who knew.

She felt weepy. She hadn't experienced these sudden bouts of tears since menopause. She went into the confectionery and bought a half-dozen lemon squares. She took the long way home. She sensed that panther was already there pacing, waiting for her, having been unleashed by that shithead Roy. Who asks someone in their sixties about their favorite lecturer from undergrad?

Nine

Lavia left the restaurant, too. She abandoned her endive and mushroom salad much the way Cynthia had run out on her burger and shake. Not because of Roy, though. Lavia didn't particularly dislike Roy. He was an average white guy like so many she'd known who didn't know how to be any other way than the way they were because they happened to be living during a time that was their time. "He's a white man in America, guys," she'd insist to Cynthia and Bloc when they complained about him.

Plus she'd witnessed his struggle. She'd seen the incident with Bloc unfold in the community room during the drive to collect gently used items to send to Puerto Rico after Hurricane Maria. Bloc had set down his plastic bag of shirts and pants that he'd just picked up from the Wash n' Fold when Roy tapped him on the shoulder and said, "Sir, you apparently didn't hear me; I'm trying to get help with some heavy boxes if you don't mind."

"Happy to help if I can," Bloc said, extending his hand. "I'm Bloc, and you are?"

"Roy," he said, without shaking Bloc's hand. "And I don't

mean to be demanding, but unless you're on a break, I could use your help like five minutes ago."

Lavia, realizing the error Roy was in the process of committing, rushed out from behind the table where'd she been organizing donations by item type. "Roy," she called, "I see you've met one of my favorite residents, Bloc." She emphasized *resident*. She was too late.

"Break? Break? Did you just ask if I was on a break? Do you think I work for you?" Bloc said, his voice rising.

Roy's face went whiter. "Oh, forgive me. Please, excuse my, my egregious error." Now Roy extended his hand.

"Man, fuck you," Bloc said, taking his voice to a whisper. "And you can keep your handshake."

"Damn, dude, you really stepped in it," Lavia said to Roy after Bloc walked away.

"I mean it was an honest mistake. He was hauling a trash bag."

"His donations, Roy, it's a drop-off event. Don't you see other people doing the same?"

"Of course. But I'm new here, and he was kind of bopping about."

"Bopping about? As in shuffling, Roy? Is that what he was doing?"

"Dear god, no, that's not what I mean." He rubbed his forehead as if he could rub away the red flushing his face. "Please don't tell Maze, she'd be mortified. And you and Bloc appear to be friends. Maybe you could put in a good word for me. Tell him I'm no bigot. I mean we've all got our implicit bias. You know, I need to work through mine."

"Yeah, like next time you see a Black man with a plastic bag filled with clean clothes in a room filled with white people lugging similar bags, don't assume that said Black man is the help. You should apologize to me, too, because I'm offended."

"I'm sorry, Lavia. My behavior was offensive to anyone with a shred of human decency."

Lavia sensed his struggle, and his sincerity. "So what's your implicit bias, say, about me?" she asked him. "Since I'm neither Black nor white, I suppose you assume I'm a doctor or a nuclear physicist?"

"Oh, so you are Indian," he joked. And then rushed to apologize again, saying he hoped he hadn't offended her twice in five minutes.

. . .

Lavia wasn't offended. She wasn't Indian, though it was easier to just let people think that she was. The truth was too complicated. That's one reason she preferred socializing with Tish and Bloc and now Cynthia. She'd say she was from everywhere and nowhere and they'd nod and pass her a joint.

She was raised on a cruise ship where her parents worked. Her father, Tui, was Indigenous Australian. He had run away from the horrors of the Kinchela Aboriginal Boys Training Home where he'd managed to survive nightly abuse after being torn from his real home due to an inhumane governmental policy of assimilation that held that First Nations children like him should be trained in the ways of white people. Tui was too brown to be adopted by a white family so he was placed in the Kinchela home to be farmed out as a laborer. After his escape, he stowed away on a ship operated by P&O, a British cruise line, and hid himself among the stored baggage. When he was discovered by the head steward, he begged the man to toss him into the ocean because its torrents would be kinder than the treatment at the home. The steward was decent and took pity. He hired Tui to trap and discard the rats that managed to circumvent the huge discs spinning freely on mooring lines. By the time Tui met Liana, Lavia's mother, he had already been promoted to an assistant steward charged with storing and retrieving the excesses that couldn't be accommodated in the guests' cabins.

Liana's circumstances were similar to Tui's but different. She had a lighter complexion so she wasn't institutionalized but instead placed for adoption with a white family, where she was more like a hand servant than a daughter to the wealthy matriarch, Elise. Liana would accompany Elise on lavish cruises where she helped her to bathe, and get in and out of her girdles, and her beaded dinner gowns. She washed and styled her hair and painted her nails to match outfits that she changed several times a day. Liana was also responsible for the selection of whatever jewelry had made the trip. Elise insisted that the pouch containing her diamonds and emeralds and rubies remain strapped around Liana's waist under her clothing at all times because she trusted neither the ocean liner's safety, nor the cabin help. She also didn't trust her physician, who'd cautioned her about her diet; she was a large woman with an appetite to match and suffered from diabetes and heart disease.

Halfway between India and Australia, during the grand Taste of the World Captain's Ball, Elise overindulged on everything offered from seafood paella, to calzone, to Peking duck, to shish kebab, to massaman curry, to pierogi, to prime rib. Later that night, after Liana had finally gotten Elise out of her one-piece girdle and bra, Elise let out a mile-long breath of relief, then succumbed to a massive heart attack.

Liana was devasted, but liberated too. With Tui's help, she pretended to disembark the ship onto the ferry that would shuttle Elise's remains back to Australia. Tui snuck Liana back onto the ship and hid her among the stored luggage and mink and sable coats where he'd hidden himself years before. He started the rumor that Liana had gone overboard, and at the next port of call, the two of them abandoned that ship and were quickly hired by the Cunard Line, Elise's jewels still secure around Liana's waist.

A year later Lavia was born aboard a ship sailing in international waters. She was born stateless but not rudderless, nurtured and fiercely protected as she was by her parents, and also by her village of stewards and kitchen aides.

Lavia took her father's stature—he was short—and his incredible cheekbones. She inherited her mother's straight hair and soft dark eyes. Lavia's golden brown complexion was a blend of the two. She was a precocious child. Her onboard education was unstructured, swathing across the world, and also deep. By her early teens she could converse with most of the workers in their native tongues. She could also approximate the accents of the travelers from Britain and the United States. She learned what she could never learn in school. Some things were based on stories her parents told her about their lives before the invaders snatched them away. Others she learned from the ocean itself, that the ocean, not the ship, is all-powerful. The ocean accommodates the ship because it can; it allows the vessel to cruise its surface and then fills in the space the ship has left as if it had never been there, that's how much it cared about the puny ocean liner. Lavia would liken the ship and its presumption of mastering the ocean to the rich white Europeans and Americans whose towels she helped her father's stewards roll—her father was the head steward by then. The pompous travelers were not nearly as smart as they thought themselves to be, but it was the thinking themselves so that gave them the edge and the power to control the narrative.

She set out to control her own narrative in her own way. She would dress up in the throwaway gowns left by the people so obscenely wealthy that they could wear a gown once and abandon it. She'd slip into a grand ball and decide one night that she was Indian royalty, another that she was on vacation from boarding school in Vermont. The boarding school became a reality. Her parents, who had been too terrified when Liana first acquired her adopted mother's jewelry to attempt to sell it, had relaxed over time. More than a decade and a half later, they traded an emerald and diamond bracelet for the opportunity to give their only child a world-class education. They enrolled her at an exclusive Massachusetts boarding school that was hungry for international-looking students like Lavia to grace the front of their glossy promotional brochures.

Lavia went on to pursue a career in finance, though she'd long ago chosen her passion job, or it had chosen her.

It started the summer between her junior and last year of high school. She'd told her boarding school friends that she was cruising the Asiatic seas. She left out the part that she'd also be working, helping her parents as she'd always done in whatever responsibilities they had on the ship. She could pick and choose her duties by then because both Tui and Liana had risen up the ranks to become senior-level staffers. She'd help her mother select the flower arrangements for the stateroom or ferry suggestions to the assistant cruise director about films they should screen. She'd had no problem donning a maid's uniform if a viral infection left them short-staffed. In the evenings, though, she'd decide who she wanted to be and play dress-up and attend the after-dinner concerts and parties and shows.

One night she met a man. He had a British accent and silvery hair and a perfect tan except for the tip of his nose, which was pink. Lavia had been watching him all week, fascinated by him because he was traveling alone and didn't seem to be on the hound for women—or even discreetly for men—the way some men traveling solo were. He was always impeccably dressed and had an easy but not especially gregarious manner. She thought he might be a hit man. He'd always seem to appear in the dining room within minutes of a Spanish couple, even though his seating was an hour later than theirs. This night as she watched him sitting at a small round table, his eyes on the couple as they danced to the orchestra's rendition of "Moon River," Lavia approached his table and asked if he minded if she had a seat there.

He said certainly he did not mind, then went back to watching the Spanish couple dance.

She started chattering then. "My feet are killing me in these heels," she said, "but thank goodness I've been fortunate to be able to shed the sari in place of a gown more suitable for walking, or dancing."

He nodded and sipped his ginger ale; she knew it was ginger ale because she'd asked Lin, the bartender for this hall, what he was drinking. "I'm accompanying my aunt on my obligatory summer cruise," she continued. "We've been doing these since I was five. And once I turned sixteen, she won't allow me to accompany her anywhere in public in nontraditional garb."

"How did you manage to escape the sari tonight?" he asked, looking at her now.

"My aunt is ailing. So she retired early."

"That's too bad," he said.

"Oh, she'll be just fine. Just a touch of motion sickness. Regardless, she's as strong as an ox."

"No, that's not what I meant. Too bad about your aunt, of course, that she is not able to be up and about, but I was actually referring to the sari. Too bad you're not wearing it because they are indeed pieces of art. The intricacies of the threads, the vibrant colors, the mix of textures—"

"That's kind of you to say, my aunt would be thrilled to hear it." She smiled demurely as she sipped her Shirley Temple. "But they can be so constricting as well."

"Hm," he said, returning her smile. It was a closed-mouth smile. "Might the sari be as constricting as the maid uniform you were wearing earlier?"

"Maid uniform? Was I, though?" she asked. Her smile

116

remained remarkably unfrozen. She didn't flinch, She didn't waver. She had no fear. This ship was loaded with staffers who'd go to the wall to keep her safe. A drunk guest once put his hand on her behind and grabbed it so hard that she yelled out in pain. Later that night he received an ornate basket of edible delights, courtesy of the crew. By the next hour he'd developed a case of diarrhea so intense that the doctor had to be summoned and he was quarantined to his cabin for the balance of the cruise lest he cause an outbreak of intestinal flu.

Lavia looked at this one straight on as he said, "Yes, you were actually in a maid's uniform this morning. And you're quite good with this little change-of-identity game you're playing. A nice addition, I'm sure, to the upcoming conversations about how I spent my summer vacation. But to be even better, you must know who's watching you. I've been watching you all week. And I know you've been watching me." He chuckled. "And you've been woefully unaware."

She focused in on his nose, the pink tip of it, and also the silver specks hanging along the shoulder of his jacket. She said, "A small bit of advice to you then." Now he was raising his brows. "You should keep your handkerchief from your nose when you've painted on your tan, and lose the black jacket if you're spraying your hair with silver dye."

He nodded, impressed with her she could tell. "So what's your deal?" she asked, dropping the accent and the affect.

"I gather intelligence."

"Like a spy?"

"Not like a spy, a spy exactly."

"Thank god, I thought you were a hit man."

"Well, Lavia, would you have told your dad, Tui, if I were?"

"If I thought innocents could be harmed, yes. But you seem as if you'd be remarkably precise, so maybe not."

"And you show no reaction that I know who you are."

"Well, you should know who I am. You claim to be a spy. I'd lose all respect for you if you didn't. So what government are you working for, or are you not allowed to say, Mr. Robert Fontbourn." She'd checked the manifest.

"Actually I'm with a private company," he said, breaking out into a grin. "And I shall not disguise my delight that you took the time to find out who I am. My company is called INI if you want to check up on me to make sure that I'm legitimate. We occasionally contract with government entities, but for the most part our clients are individuals or companies or corporations that need intelligence."

"Are you supposed to be revealing this?" she asked.

"I'm free to, yes. Though I'm also discreet. I'm only telling you because I'd like to enlist your help. It's a short, simple task, and I think lucrative for someone like you, a high school student who spends her summer off from boarding school helping out her parents by serving as a maid. Which I honestly find quite endearing."

Lavia would have done it for free; it was so easy, but so thrilling, too. Retrieve a document from the Spanish man's cabin, a blueprint, and replace it with a look-alike. She imagined the intensity of the experience was akin to what her classmates described when they'd let a boy feel them up: the anticipation;

118

the pounding heart as she waited for the couple to go to the upper deck for cocktails the way they did every afternoon; the casually taking the master key from the wall behind Tui's desk as he hunched over grids containing schedules and calendars and she leaned down to kiss the top of his balding head, telling him there was a lockout, but she would handle it; the stepping into the cabin, stepping into the couple's world, stealing the air in there that was their air—it was intoxicating as the tension built, as the pleasure on top of pleasure built, so good, like a thousand feathers stroking. And then the climax that was simultaneously focused and scattered moving through her as she held the thin sheets of paper between her fingers. It was a feeling she knew she'd crave again and again. And in that moment she knew what she wanted to do, to be. A spy.

. . .

So when Lavia saw a text from Robert—her first mentor, her sometimes lover, forever friend—glowing on her phone as she sat in the Throwback's soft leather booth and listened to Cynthia and Tish tussle over whether or not it mattered that Roy found *Girls Trip* interesting, she assumed he wanted to entice her with a job. She was mostly retired, but she'd occasionally take on an assignment that aroused that part of her that was turbulent like the ocean. Robert wasn't trying to talk her into a project, though. He had visited with her father earlier. *He doesn't want to worry you, but he's not well. You should come.* The *you should come* part stopped her breath, even as her heart pounded double time. She quickly gathered herself and told Roy and Tish that she had to leave too.

"Milkshake got to you as well?" Roy asked.

"I didn't have a milkshake, and no, Roy, you're not scaring me off like you didn't scare Cynthia off," she said. "I've got business to handle."

"Thanks," Tish whispered as she moved out of the booth so Lavia could scoot past. Lavia hunched her shoulders as if asking, *thanks for what?* Tish winked and Lavia realized that Tish thought she was leaving so abruptly to give Tish and Roy alone time in that booth. Lavia felt a sudden storm of anger gathering in her chest. She knew that Tish had been with Roy before. Tish had blushed like a teenager when she'd described for Lavia how Roy had dropped by when Maze had traveled to DC for the climate march. "A onetime thing," she'd told Lavia. "He was telling me about the horrors of the emergency appendectomy he'd had the year before and I don't know why I asked to see the scar, but I did, and he lifted up his shirt to show me. I rubbed my fingers along the length of that raised skin, and then, what can I say, that's all she wrote."

"If you don't know why you asked to see the scar," Lavia had said, mildly repulsed by the dreamy expression on Tish's face, "then, to use your favorite phrase, you got issues, girl."

Lavia walked to the pond and sat on a bench next to where a willow leaned toward the water as if stretching to take a drink. She breathed the air in slowly that smelled of lilies and wet earth. She counted as she breathed, in for four, hold for four, out for four, hold for four. She listened to the splashing sounds the ducks made. She was trying to let go of her anger. It wasn't that Tish was having an affair with an old married guy that had Lavia so incensed. It was that Tish's level of self-absorption was so out-sized that it rendered Tish incapable of considering that Lavia's sudden departure in the middle of her salad had nothing to do with Tish.

She also knew that her anger, real as it was, was also a deflection. She was terrified of losing her father. She'd lost her mother five years before and had prepared herself for her father's passing in the months that immediately followed. They'd both been so hollowed out by Liana's death, but Lavia knew she would walk through her grief, like the dark tunnel it was, toward the light. She was certain that her father would not, that he would die of a broken heart. To her amazement, he'd rallied. And she'd allowed herself to revert to her childish mind that believed in the impossible, that he would live forever.

She picked up her phone and read Robert's text again. "Oh, Mah-mah," she said to the pond and the tree and the ducks. The ducks seemed to turn to look at her as they flapped their wings. "Hold on, Mah-mah, I'm coming," she said, as she closed out the text message and booked the next flight she could get to Sydney. She would leave in the morning.

Ten

Cynthia was on the commuter train headed into Philly. She had the song in her head about wishing it would rain to hide her teardrops, but the weather didn't yield to her wish this day. It was perfect weather for anyone not going to a funeral, or the hospital to visit a sick loved one, or to sign papers that meant from this day forward, her house was no longer her house.

A brilliant September sun ushered her to the realtor's office, seventy-five degrees with low humidity, a light breeze, and low pollen count because it had rained torrents the day before. She wished the closing had been yesterday; it seemed more appropriate to be walking through mud puddles that smelled of dog shit, not this ground that felt crunchy underfoot, like mounds of shredded wheat topped with brown sugar sweetening the air.

E and Melanie met her at the closing, dressed for the pomp and circumstance and also because they were taking her to a nice lunch afterward. When Melanie said nice lunch, Cynthia knew that was code for dressing up, so she was suited down, wide-heeled pumps, pearls, and her twist-out that was fresh and crinkly. Their realtor was E's childhood friend, giving Cynthia yet another thing to miss about her house: splattering sounds and laughter coming from her kitchen most afternoons when she'd been able to work half days from home before such arrangements were common, and she would open her house and endless jars of peanut butter and jelly to E's friends who'd otherwise be latchkey kids.

E and Melanie flanked her in the office's high-backed wooden chairs that Cynthia thought should be at somebody's dining room table, in somebody's dining room, the room with the chandelier throwing white light that should be the setting for Thanksgiving. She could almost taste eggnog as she sipped the freshly brewed coffee heavy with cream. They were selling to a young white couple pregnant with their first child. Cynthia was happy and sad about that. Happy because they were young and kind and her house would again experience the joys of new love, the promise of new life. Sad because she wished they were Black because the neighborhood would shortly be all white and she was contributing to that. E had insisted that Cynthia's hesitation to sign the agreement because the couple was white was wrong, just wrong, legally, morally, and was also racist, because it was rejecting an offer based solely on race.

"You need to know where I'm coming from," she'd countered. "That nice young couple with their 800 credit score and generational wealth will do just fine. Somebody like your dad and I, saddled back then with student loan debt and needing to go FHA because we'd barely managed to save five percent for the down payment, would not have been in a position to go above asking."

E had softened then, saying he got it, he really got it. Though she knew he really didn't. He'd been a child whose close friends mimicked a bazaar of all nations, so he was genuinely confused when she'd tell stories of undergrad and once described how all the Black people sat together in the dining hall. "Why?" he'd asked.

When they were touring the Gen, she'd queried the sales associate about other buyers: "Are any of them Black? What proportion?"

"Mom, you know he can't answer that," E said, stopping her. "That's in violation of the Fair Housing Act. It doesn't matter anyhow if you like the place."

"If you knew from what I knew, it would matter," she'd said. Though she also had to concede that she and Ethrow had done their part based on Khalil Gibran's writings about a parent's duty to prepare their children for a world they (the parents) can never go to, not even in their dreams.

They chatted with the couple before the signings began. The husband said how much he loved the block. The wife talked about the interior features like the arched foyer. Cynthia flashed back to the sudsy feel the house would take on during the grand gatherings she and Ethrow hosted in support of rising political stars. She was seeing the foyer where they'd linger and hold parting conversations as their guests left. She was remembering how the chandelier threw its brightness against the crown molding that bled into the living room because that's all she could see that night after she'd witnessed her marriage disassemble in that foyer when Ethrow's coworker, lithe and leggy in six-inch heels and a mile-long weave, forgot where she was after too much champagne and kissed his lips good night instead of the usual cordial hug.

"It is an incredible foyer," Cynthia said, and she prayed a silent prayer for the young couple that their marriage not succumb to the inevitable storms.

She got through the settlement with nary a tear. E and Melanie shifted closer and closer to her with each page she signed until their shoulders were actually restricting her and she remembered a story Gabriella told her about her cousin's funeral when the wife was escorted up to the casket for the final viewing and the undertakers, one on each side, were stuck so close to her that she finally pulled away; pushed one, then the other, shouting *get the fuck off me so I can say my goodbyes*. Gabriella said the crying throughout the church turned to bawling laughter and that was just what they all needed. It was what Cynthia needed at the moment, too, as she imagined that scene and signed the last page and watched the casket lid close softly on her house.

Cynthia had expected the nice lunch to be at a stodgy place like Prime Rib or the Palm so she was ecstatic when they headed west instead of east, up Baltimore Avenue. They lucked out on a parking space in front of Booker's, one of her favorite restaurants in her now former neighborhood that was a panoply of noise and accents and aromas and people. "Oh guys, thank you," she said as they held the door for her to enter and already she was thinking of the restaurant's macaroni and cheese.

E and Melanie kept looking at her, and then glancing at each other even as they all devoured their meals. And finally Cynthia said, "Okay, guys, signing my house away was difficult for me, very difficult. But I'll get through it, plus I've got a few extra dollars in my bank account—"

"Uh, quite a bit many more than a few," E said.

"Okay, granted. I'm feeling kina rich for the moment. So you can stop giving each other the is-she-all-right look. I promise, I'm not about to cry my eyes out here and now, especially not over this fried chicken."

"Well, I don't know, Mom," E said, "after we tell you what we have to tell you." He reached into his jacket pocket and pulled out a folded handkerchief. *His dad was never without a handkerchief, either*, she thought, trying to stay with the thought of what a good father Ethrow had been, as she felt her heart racing about whatever it was E was preparing to say.

The handkerchief was white with pink and blue teddy bears holding pink and blue hearts. She looked at Melanie, who was tearing up and smiling, and E was just smiling, now laughing and nodding, now his eyes were filling up and spilling over too.

"Oh dear god," Cynthia said. "Oh, oh, oh, give me the damn handkerchief." She covered her face and sobbed. They surrounded her on either side again, this time a good surround as she cried so hard that her back shook. She cried for the house she'd just let go of, the baby swimming in Melanie's womb, the cycle of life and death that was irrefutable, hard but fair as her grandmother used to say. And she was at the hard part of accepting that she'd lived more of her years than she had left to live. But the soft part was coming. A baby. She stood from her seat and threw her hands up, announcing, "I'm gonna be a grandmother." The lunch crowd of students and neighborhood folk, doctors, politicians, people who worked at the bank, the community organization, the university, and the lawyers and executives who'd made the trek from Center City for a soul food lunch all applauded. She pulled E and Melanie to her and they hugged and swayed. That sway was so good it felt like church when the clap-to choir sang.

Eleven

Cynthia had started bringing food to the regular weed-smoking, wine-drinking, dancing or card-playing, movie-watching or storytelling nights at Tish's cottage that sometimes lasted until the morning because they'd all fall asleep. She loved the way they swooned over her cooking: the macaroni and cheese burned on the top the way her grandmother made it; the roasted turkey wings smothered in the dumplings she'd fashioned from pizza dough; the rainbow trout sautéed in avocado oil and garlic. Tonight she would be bringing the roasted-to-perfection lemon and sage chicken thighs dusted with almond flour so that the skin had a heavenly crunch and the meat was so tender it practically melted.

She sampled a piece; it was not quite as perfect as her grandmother's who'd considered it blasphemous to bake anything without a glaze of lard, but it was still slap your mama good, as Bloc would say about everything she'd cooked thus far.

Not cooking for you, Mister Mister, she said to herself right now, borrowing Tish's nickname for Bloc. Still, as she worked her way through the skin of the chicken thigh to get to the meat that was just-right juicy, she imagined Bloc's expression when he tasted it tonight. He'd close his eyes lightly and the muscles in his face would slacken as if a dab of heaven had landed on his tongue; he'd let go an almost imperceptible moan, a subtle, shortened version of the moaning sounds he'd pushed in her ear that afternoon when he'd gotten her high and taken her to her air mattress, or she'd taken him.

As she finished the chicken and reapplied her lipstick and adjusted her velvet top so that it fell from her shoulders just so, Cynthia pushed thoughts of him from her mind again, reminding herself that that one time had been months ago. She told herself, too, that she wasn't dressing up for him, either, the same way she told herself when she danced across Tish's great room, twisting her waist that was small, and sashaying her hips that were wide, that she was not dancing for Bloc; the same way she told herself that when she won a hand at pinochle and jumped up and down and twirled, even though she threatened to throw her back out, that the twirl was not for Bloc; the same way she told herself right now as she pulled her fingers through her hair, to get her 'fro to stand as wide and as high as she could, that she was not fashioning her hair for Bloc, even as she remembered the feel of his hands through her hair as he'd kissed her face and whispered *ooh, ooh, baby, baby*, saying how much he loved her hair. "Not fanning my hair out for you, Mr. Bloc, hell no," she said out loud, as she looked at herself in the mirror, herself looking back at her with a smirk that said, *Girl, please.*

Cynthia sighed as she washed her hands and used tongs to remove the chicken from the pan and arranged it on her rainbow-colored, oval-shaped tray already lined with leaves of fresh sage and lemon slices. She resisted counting the chicken pieces lest she have her grandmother's voice in her head warning her that it was bad luck to count food, meant you didn't trust that God would make it all be enough. But Tish had texted her not long ago alerting her that the size of the gathering would likely double tonight because she'd invited other people to join them. Cynthia didn't ask who. She was excited, though, that Lavia, who'd been away for the past six weeks, would finally be in the mix again. She'd really missed her.

She wound her cashmere wrap over her shoulders and arms, the wrap a Christmas gift from Tish. She balanced the tray loaded with the chicken thighs as she walked to Tish's. She could still taste the lemon and the sage from the chicken she'd sampled. She smelled the pine needles that crunched under her high but wide-heeled boots. When she saw Bloc ahead of her, she started to slow her steps so he could go on in, but then she called out to him instead. "Bloc, can you help me with this tray, please?" She watched him turn, and smile, and walk toward her. He was in an olive-colored suede jacket and matching turtleneck. She wondered if the jacket and sweater had been a Christmas gift from Tish. She was glad at least he wasn't wearing gingham under the jacket.

• • •

Tish's dining table was shaped like a grand fried egg where the edges splattered out from the yolk and curved and indented and curlicued. She'd bought it as a piece of art from a craft fair and turned it into a dining table by having it secured to a base; it could seat a dozen people. She liked that the table had no designated head spot. Her father had always sat at the head of the table, her mother at the other end. Though as carefree as Tish was in her relationships, she forbade the man the head spot. Reasoned that it was unresolved anger at her father for dying on them in the most undignified way possible. *At a whorehouse? Really, Daddy?* She'd say the words out loud when she was alone, and the thought came to her now in a sudden thud that she felt at the top of her head, but also in her heart.

She was finding it increasingly difficult not to think about him since she'd moved to the Philly area and had been spending time with her cousins. Her cousins talked about him constantly. "That's Uncle Gord right there," one or the other would say when Tish smirked, or opened her eyes wide when something amazed her, or pursed her lips in anger, or said yeah, yeah, yeah in rapid succession if she agreed with what had just been said. They'd try to explain to Tish that it wasn't just that they missed him, it was that his death, the official circumstances of it, could not be not true. They'd tried to convince Tish over the years that her father could have been set up, murdered for all they knew, retaliated against because of his provocative views.

"I'm not saying Uncle Gord was a saint," Gordenia had said when she'd visited Tish the week before. "But a prostitute. No, no, no, no, no. I said it then and I say it now. I do not believe that's how he died. I will never believe that's how he died. Nor should you, Natasha— I mean Tish Jones. Nor should you."

Tish would get a chill whenever one or the other of her cousins slipped up and called her by her birth name, Natasha. Remnants, she thought, of her reaction when she'd gotten official notification that the legalities of the name change had been satisfied, that she would from then on be known as Tish Jones. Her body felt cold that day and she began to shake uncontrollably, convulsively. That had happened to her once when she was a child and had a high fever and after she'd recovered her father explained that it was just her body protecting her, it needed to heat up to fight the virus, but it couldn't get too hot, so it had to cool itself down quickly, and it was the cooling down that caused the chills. She thought the name change was bringing down the heat on her grief and humiliation about the way he died. Everything had been happening so quickly then, her move to Virginia with her mother, her preparation for college and relocation to the West Coast, leaving her cousins and her aunt, leaving her true self: that cute little girl who went out of her way to discover the beauty in other people, and to point it out to them at every turn because that's what her father had taught her.

Tish didn't know which was more unsettling after conversations with her cousins, the possibility that someone had hurt her father or the reality that he'd died in the thrill of some prostitute's embrace. Ultimately, the conspiracy theory talk made it too difficult for her to move on, so she buried the idea of it, like she'd buried the idea of him.

But lately she'd feel a tug growing into a yearning to open the door on the sequestered parts of herself. She thought it was a natural inclination as she aged to begin to slowly cast off unnecessary baggage, making it easier for her to take her inevitable flight up to the other side of the clouds whenever that time came. She thought that physics was the determinant of who went to heaven or hell. Those who'd managed to rid themselves of the weight of what no longer served them could more easily soar. Those laden by their inability to discard their garbage parts might try, but they would be unable to sustain flight and would come crashing back down and down, falling through the earth's crust to the underside with all the other bloated souls.

Tish was tussling with the consideration that maintaining that her father was a shameless whoremonger was garbage thinking. Though she hadn't yielded to figuring out how she might repair his legacy for his nieces, and for herself, she'd not slammed the door on it either.

· · ·

Lavia was debating whether or not to go to Tish's this evening. She was jet-lagged and also blue, traveling that erratic line of grief with its sharp dips and peaks. Plus Robert had accompanied her back to Philly. She invited him to stay with her, but he insisted on getting a hotel. "Enjoy your time with your friends. I'm just a text away," he said, as he loaded her bags in the trunk of the Lyft.

She watched him walk away, still fine even in his seventies, she thought, looking every bit as intriguing as he had that night on the ship when she'd pretended to be Indian royalty. They'd been good together when they were together. During graduate school in her twenties, then the middle of her thirties after his divorce, in her forties when he landed a major contract that involved counterintelligence and he pleaded with her to join the enterprise because she was the only person he knew who could become what the mission required. They were together for almost five years that time.

She'd date all kinds of men between her spates of romance with Robert. Men from different races and countries and cultures: monied, broke, serious, intellectual, jokesters, atheists, people in recovery, people who did cocaine, people who worked at Starbucks, and on Wall Street, and on K Street. She'd never fallen in love with them, never even became infatuated. She considered it independent study. She had an insatiable need to understand things. They taught her with their middle-of-the-night stories in their depleted and honest just-had-sex states. It was a one-way trip, though. She didn't reveal much about herself. Robert, though, knew her; he knew her parents, her upbringing, her world. She'd always loved him as a result. And the past month, she'd needed him, too.

She'd been shocked at how frail Tui was. His skin hung as if it said *I'm already dead, why bother remaining attached to these bones?* How did he go from the plump, robust man he was six months ago when she'd seen him last to this wasted-away version of himself? Why hadn't she noticed in their weekly FaceTimes? "He was good at hiding it," Robert said. "I only knew something was amiss when he declined my lunch invitation. Tui never declines lunch."

"Oh, Mah-mah, do you hurt? I don't want you to hurt," Lavia said, as she sat on the floor and laid her head on his thigh.

He patted her head. "It look much worst that the truth of it," he said. "But no hospice, Lavi, no hospice."

"Well, tell me what you want then, okay, whatever you want, just tell me what you want."

He said that he wanted the sea. The sea had freed him from his torture at the Kinchela Aboriginal Boys Training Home, had introduced him to his true love, Liana, had been the birthplace of his cherished daughter. The sea had given him his life, such a life. "Where else should I be when my spirit takes passage into the afterlife?" he said in a raspy voice. "Only the sea."

Lavia gave him his sea. She booked them a cruise, the highest tier of first-class accommodations so that he could be waited on, fussed over, referred to as "sir" a hundred times a day. At last, she was able to see him receive the treatment that he'd dispensed so generously for all those decades.

Just before dawn on the last day, she took him to the upper deck. She rubbed his hands with ochre. His breath came in heaves as he struggled to take in air. As the ship passed the area closest to New South Wales where Tui was born, Lavia administered the vial of morphine. The sky cracked open at that moment to accommodate a sunrise that was so bodacious, brilliant, and loud, as if James Brown were sashaying across the sky hollering *I feel good*. She thought that she saw her mah-mah smile. And just like that he was gone.

Robert organized a dinner for Tui's friends who had been like his extended family over the years. Most were from his decades working cruise ships. Many Lavia remembered from childhood. They were Philippine, and Indian, Maori. They crowded into

Tui's island home done up like the hull of a ship with muraled walls that mimicked the ornate interiors of the cruise ships he'd worked. They danced and sang and drank and ate and told outrageous stories. They laughed so hard that Lavia forgot that she was sad, then she laughed even harder realizing that was the point. She'd catch a glimpse of Robert looking at her, enjoying that she was enjoying herself. Ultimately, it was a grand time befitting the memory of a son of the First Peoples of Australia.

. . .

Lavia decided to go to Tish's after all. She'd missed them. As she was zipping her ankle boots her phone pinged with a text from Robert and she thought he might say he'd changed his mind, he wanted to come and spend time with her at the Gen. She was disappointed that he wasn't saying that, and then disappointed in herself for being disappointed because she didn't want to fall into a traditional relationship with him. She thought the fluid nature of their together time was like plunging deep into the sea, enabling them to be constantly fascinated by what they could never discover by just looking at the surface waves. They'd come up for air then, because of course they had to. She was fearful they'd drown each other if it were any other way.

She scanned his text quickly, and then stood there in one boot to read it thoroughly after the sentence *Interesting tidbit on your friend Tish*. They were still doing that, glimpsing into the backgrounds of the other's new friends. More of a game between them than a deep dive investigation because the friend aroused suspicion. She'd once discovered a friend of Robert's from London, a Nigerian woman who Lavia thought had the face of a goddess, and who she assumed had had thousands of dollars of work done, had actually been unhoused for more than two years. That fact had endeared the woman to Lavia.

Lavia clicked on the attachments included with Robert's text. One was the police report about the death of Gordon Willis in 1973. Gordon had been a Black scholar, and had spent the days prior to his death lecturing on campuses in the Philadelphia area. He'd been found unresponsive in the early morning hours on the front porch of a known Philadelphia brothel. The next attachment was dated a month after Gordon's death—Tish's petition to change her name from Natasha Willis to Tish Jones.

Lavia was not entirely surprised that the disgraced-in-death Gordon Willis was Tish's father. Tish's conversation had always turned cloudy when the subject of fathers came up. Such a contrast to her open-book, turn-my-pages, read-me, read-all-of-me affect. Lavia understood that. She'd been guarded about her own parents. She'd had to be. Her parents had, after all, faked Liana's death, then acquired and then sold the jewels of Liana's foster mother/enslaver—as Lavia referred to her—to educate Lavia. And although Tui and Liana grew less tormented over the years that they'd be discovered, Lavia vowed that as long as her parents were alive, she'd protect them by remaining vague about who she was, where she was from; she'd always considered it an act of solidarity, an act of love. She thought Tish had done the opposite.

Tish had disavowed her father by deleting him from her life.

But not to benefit him, to benefit her. Not to protect his well-being, but to protect her image. "Damn, Tish," she said out loud as she stepped into her other boot and then stomped her foot in anger. "I mean, damn, Tish," she repeated, "just damn."

She tried to move from her judgmental self, tried to call up empathy to feel what Tish must have felt to motivate her to change her name. Had she not just lost Tui, perhaps she would have been more forgiving. But she was still aching over her loss. Her loss was still too fresh, too immense.

Twelve

When Lavia got to Tish's, Cynthia and Bloc were already there. They practically knocked each other over to get to her, to hug her, talking on top of one another saying how much they'd missed her, how was she, how was the funeral, they would have sent flowers but they had not a clue where to send them. And then asking how was she all over again. "You think you can prepare for it when you know it's imminent," Bloc said, "but it's impossible to prepare for someone you love being dead while they're still alive."

"Right?" Cynthia said, helping Lavia out of her coat. "I lost my mom five years ago, and I still think about her every single day. And we had our ups and downs, 'cause she was bipolar."

"Well, look at you with the gallows humor, Cynthia, ups and downs, bipolar," Lavia said. "I see you've been holding down the fort in my absence."

"She hasn't really," Tish said. "You're too irreplaceable." She pulled Lavia in for a long hug, and part of Lavia wanted to push Tish away, but a larger part of her needed to hold on.

They appeared to fall back into their usual rhythms, their

easy ways of being together, snarking at one another, then soothing over the insults, making each other laugh as if Lavia hadn't been away the past month and a half. Except that Lavia knew that she had been away, knew that she was in odd spaces right now in her head and in her heart. She tried to keep her normal self, the Lavia they were accustomed to, from sliding away to some unrecapturable abyss as Cynthia passed around her phone showing off pictures of Melanie's latest ultrasound. "Look at my grand-fetus," she gushed.

"Definitely has your eyes," Lavia said to laughter.

"Oh my god, I have got to show y'all the newest pictures of Shisha's child. Y'all remember Shisha, my cousin's daughter, GG's child," Tish said, as she scrolled through her phone. "She's named for me—"

"We know," Lavia said. "How many times have we heard that she's the one who acts more like you than you do."

"Truth," Tish said, "I'm amazed she's settled down enough to marry and have a child of her own. And she knows everything. She's the one who suggested I lock my hair; now whenever I see her, first thing out of her mouth is, 'Auntie, aren't you glad you took my advice about the hair?'"

"They all know everything at that age," Cynthia said.

"But sometimes they give amazingly astute counsel," Tish said, as she cooed at her phone. "I guess I knew everything, too, when I was that age."

"That age, this age," Lavia said, as she took the phone and barely glanced at it, and said "Cute," and handed it to Cynthia.

"Aw, that is one beautiful baby," Cynthia said.

"I'm not biased when I say that is the most absolute gorgeous baby born to womankind—" Tish said.

"Until Cynthia's grandchild is born," Lavia interrupted.

Bloc looked at the phone and said, "Gorgeous; she's grown quite a bit since I saw her just a couple of weeks ago."

"Babies do tend to grow, Bloc," Lavia said, then wrestled the focus of the conversation away from Tish and asked Cynthia if she still loved it here at the Gen the way she'd said she did the last time they actually sat down and talked back when they'd gone to the Throwback after the movies that afternoon. "Feels like a lifetime ago, Cynthia, but are you still in that positive space about living here?"

"Aw, thanks for asking" Cynthia said. "And it was a lifetime ago for you because your life separated around then into one of those before, after demarcations."

Lavia nodded, appreciating the acknowledgment as Cynthia said that yes, it has remained good for her. "My dear know-it-all son was quite accurate when he likened my abhorrence for this place to his going to sleepaway summer camp, and how after hating camp at first, it suddenly got good for him. I was so pissed when he said that, like this is no effing camp. This is a permanent separation from life as I knew it. But now"—she broke out into a broad grin—"I have so enjoyed these evenings with you guys. And I haven't played this much pinochle since undergrad."

"Or smoked this much weed," Lavia said.

"That too." She touched Bloc's hand when she said that. "Appreciate you and your, as you call him, your young boy for that, Bloc. And then there's also the setting; you know, the open feel of this place, the trees, the lake, the creek, the pastoral nature of it. The sunrises, the quiet. And yeah, the being with people my own age. I mean the world is so young, especially where I lived so close to a college campus."

"That's the least of it for me," Lavia said, "being with people my own age."

"That's 'cause you're short, Lavia," Tish said.

Lavia put her glass down and glared at Tish. "That's a really mean thing to say, Tish."

"No, I didn't intend it as an insult, honestly," Tish said. "Your height makes you look young. Seriously, people always thought I was two, three years older than I was because of my height."

"Height aside, you do look damn young, Lavia," Bloc said. "When I first met you, I was, like, how they let this young girl move in? They clearly didn't ask for proof of age before they let you buy here."

"Maybe I am young, maybe I lied," Lavia said.

"Who the hell would lie to live around a bunch of senior citizens?" Tish asked.

"People lie for all kinds of reasons," Lavia said. "Who they are, where they're from—who's their daddy. You should know that better than anyone, Tish."

"What the hell is that supposed to mean?" Tish said, jerking her glass away and spilling champagne on her top. "Shit—" She jumped up, wiping her top with her hands.

"I tell you what," Bloc said, trying to diffuse the apparent storm brewing between Lavia and Tish, "I'm ready for some music, and that sage chicken Cynthia cooked sitting in that warming drawer is calling my name."

"I'm with you on the music, Bloc," Cynthia said.

"Bloc, you deejay, I got to change," Tish said as she moved toward her bedroom.

Bloc picked up Tish's phone and Cynthia noted that he scrolled through the phone as if it were his. "Okay, I'm honoring requests. I know you want James Brown, Lavia."

"Actually, I'm in the mood for some Patti LaBelle; how about 'Lady Marmalade'?"

"Hmm . . ." Bloc raised his eyebrows and smiled. "I'm liking your selection," he said, as Patti LaBelle singing the opening line—hey sister, soul sister—of "Lady Marmalade" rained down. "That's what I'm talking about." He extended his hand to Lavia. "Come on, soul sister in your own right, dance with me."

"I'm so tired, my dear soul brother Bloc, my soul sister Cynthia will pick up the slack," Lavia said, as she took Bloc's extended hand and placed it on Cynthia's arm.

Cynthia stood and Bloc's eyes fell to Cynthia's hips where they always wanted to go anyhow, but out of politeness he'd mostly manage to keep his focus above her neck. He averted his gaze quickly as he backed up; the farther back he went, the more Cynthia danced toward him. He tried to dance then, but his moves felt stilted. His guilt, he knew. Since their time together on her air mattress, he'd waited for any sliver of an opening so that he could explain his egregious behavior. The way he'd ghosted her, as his young boy would say. He'd told himself that he'd never had the opportunity to explain himself, not wanting to admit that he'd not taken it upon himself to create an opportunity.

Cynthia picked up the rhythm easily as she swayed her hips in sync with her shoulders. She moved in and out with cha-cha steps and sang out loud the part that asks, *hey Joe, wanna give it a go?* She looked right at Bloc as she sang. Watched him avoid looking at her, his eyes on his feet as if he had to see his feet to make them move. And his moves right now were wooden, relative to his free form when she'd watched him dance with other people. The song was approaching the part when Patti LaBelle asks in French, in the sultriest of voices, *Do you want to sleep with me tonight?* Cynthia didn't know what was prompting her behavior right now as she prepared to fix her face in that expression that she'd seen on her mother's face countless times in the company of one man or another. One of Divine's perfectly arched brows would tilt up ever so slightly, even as her eyes went half-mast. Her lips would hint at a pout, a smile, as if she were saying *shh.* Cynthia had never fixed her face so, except for that night with Mr. Z , though she wasn't really sure if she had then, or if Mr. Z had just convinced her that she had. But right now, with her back to the center island so that only Bloc could see her face, Cynthia was prepared to own the do-you-want-to-sleep-with-me-tonight look. Not entirely sure that she even wanted that, maybe the real pleasure was just seeing Bloc squirm. She was succeeding, applauding herself as the awkward air falling over him grew impenetrable.

Except that the music stopped, all of a sudden, before Patti could even sing *Voulez-vous.* If the sound had been coming from an album spinning on a turntable and not streaming as it was, Cynthia thought she would have heard the needle scrape hard against the vinyl, that's how abruptly the music stopped.

"I hate this damn song," Tish snapped, as all eyes turned to her.

"Well, that's a relief. I thought you were about to force us into a game of freeze/thaw, and I wasn't trying to hold a pose," Bloc said, as he made his way back to the center-island counter like a man running into the house to outrun a storm.

"And I thought you were trying to save Bloc 'cause I was about to dance circles around him," Cynthia said.

"What's wrong with the song?" Lavia asked.

"Who wants to hear about a damn prostitute coming on to a prospective john?" Tish snapped.

"Don't hate Lady Marmalade, hate the Joe giving it a go," Lavia said. "Sex workers are some of the most exploited laborers in the country."

"They're hoes, Lavia." Tish practically spit the word out.

"Well, they couldn't be hoes if they didn't have a ready and willing clientele just dying to procure their services," Lavia said.

"You sound a damn fool, Lavia," Tish said, as she moved the plates from the counter where they sat and practically slammed them down on the egg-shaped table.

Cynthia and Bloc exchanged looks asking each other what was going on between Lavia and Tish. Each hunched their shoulders in reply to the other. "Yo, yo, yo," Bloc said then. "Let's have some weed and turn the temperature down in here a few degrees."

"Well, you got to make it quick, 'cause Roy and Maze are on the way over," Tish said, as she spread napkins on the table.

"Roy and Maze . . . what the fuck, Tish," Bloc said, and then tried to call back the what the fuck, but it was out there. "You know how I feel about Roy, damn, you coulda told me, I would have passed on coming over tonight."

"Honestly, I wouldn't have come either," Cynthia said, resisting the temptation to put her hand on Bloc's arm to calm him down.

"Damn, guys, I'm sorry," Tish said.

"Are you really?" Lavia asked, coating her tone with sarcasm.

"Actually, yes, I am. They're bringing Antwon."

"Antwon?" they said in unison.

"Well, why didn't you say something when we first arrived," Lavia more accused than asked.

"You know what, Lavia—"

"It's cool, it's cool." Bloc cut Tish off before she could say more, rushing his words, to try and thin out the accreting tension between Lavia and Tish. "I didn't realize Antwon was coming. Wow. I'd love to see him, even if I have to pay the considerable cost of Roy's stuffy-ass company."

"And Maze is also good compensation. What time will they be here?" Cynthia asked.

"Around seven," Tish said. "And I really am sorry for not giving you guys a heads-up, I just wanted to surprise you, even if Lavia doesn't believe me, right, girl"—she hit Lavia's arm playfully—"Forgive me, please."

Lavia didn't move her shoulder away from the feel of Tish's

hand. She just rolled her eyes. She knew that her reaction to Tish right now had everything to do with her own grief because Tish was being who she'd always been. Except Lavia, right now, was not who she usually was. What she was feeling, thinking, emanated not from the usual places, but the new places the grief's sharp edges had discovered. Her thoughts and feelings had a rawness, but also a new depth to them. When she'd laughed since Tui died, it had been the deepest of laughs, her crying had been more ferocious than ever before, and now, her anger toward Tish burned hotter than she thought possible, especially given what she'd just learned. She knew she was being unfair to Tish, judging her based on intelligence that she hadn't even gathered, and certainly wasn't looking for, that she'd acquired only as a result of a game she and Robert had been playing with each other for years. She'd always had the ability to compartmentalize, to store that kind of intelligence in her rational mind so that it didn't seep into the part of her where emotions formed. But she'd lost the ability to do that right now. She didn't feel in control of her emotions, her thoughts fueling those emotions. She thought she should leave.

But right then Tish blurted, "Oh shit, they're here."

"Here?" Bloc said. He'd just fired up his pipe loaded with hash, the chunk of hash and the shavings and his switchblade strewn on the counter.

"Yeah, they're back there, at the end of my redbrick road," Tish said, as she stood in the middle of her great room surrounded by windows that looked out on the woods coveting her cottage. She'd had the path bricked out a full tenth of a mile leading to her house on the opposite side of the driveway.

"Redbrick road, what is that, some variation on *The Wiz?*" Lavia tried to make a joke, as she also tried to steady herself.

"Yeah? If so," Bloc said, as he snuffed his pipe, "I'm the cowardly Lion till I get rid of my contraband 'cause I don't put it beyond Roy to make a citizen's arrest. I mean, weed may be decriminalized in Philly, but we're outside of Philly at the moment. Shit, I thought you said about seven, Tish."

"Come on, Bloc," Lavia said. "You know white people consider themselves late if they arrive at the about-time. On time for them is half hour prior, so it's six thirty. They're likely pleased with themselves for their punctuality."

Tish hurriedly grabbed a scented candle from the mirrored shelf and set it in the center of the counter and Bloc lit it. Cynthia pulled the sage chicken from the warming drawer and uncovered it. "The sage from this will help," she said.

"What can I do, Tish?" Lavia asked. "How about if you just stand at the door and offer Roy brandy as they enter. I see it on your bar cart so I'm assuming it's there because that's what Roy drinks. He won't smell a thing else once that hits his nose."

"My girl Lavia does not miss a detail," Bloc said as he pressed his thumb over his pipe, making sure it was out, then dumped the ash down the sink.

"I've got macaroni and cheese and roasted zucchini in the oven that can come out," Tish said, as she poured brandy into two glasses. She opened the door then, apologizing to her new guests that her app suddenly stopped working, so it took her a minute to get to the door.

"Well, I'm old enough to remember when we actually had to walk to the door to open it as you just did," Roy said, "so for this retro moment I am profoundly grateful." He bowed slightly as Tish ushered them in.

Bloc joined Tish at the door. He extended his hand. "Roy, hello," he said.

"Why, Bloc, what a treat," Roy said as he grabbed Bloc's hand and held on.

Bloc pulled his hand away and exchanged pleasantries with Maze, and then he grabbed Antwon in a bear hug. "Damn, it's good to see you. Man, I mean damn, really so good to see you."

Antwon was tall and he leaned his head down when he stepped into the room as if out of habit and Bloc thought he must have spent too much time in low-ceilinged places because the ceilings here stretched to the clouds. He wondered about the ceiling height in prison. "It's good to be seen, Mr. Bloc," Antwon said. They moved into the great room and Maze commented on the wonderful floors and the art and the colors.

"Is that a Bearden?" Roy asked as he pointed to the print over the coral-colored vegan leather couch.

"No, I think that's Kehinde Wiley, right?" Maze said.

Tish smiled and nodded, and Roy said, "Well, of course she's right, she's right about everything," as he smooched Maze's cheek.

"I remember I helped you hang it, Miss Tish," Antwon said.

"You know who else remembers? My cousin's youngest

daughter who was supposed to be helping me unpack, but instead spent the entire time ogling over you," Tish said, and they all laughed as Tish waved her hand around the great room, telling them to have a seat, anywhere. "Me casa you casa, as my friends who have been pressed into service will tell you."

Bloc went to the bar and retrieved the glasses Tish had poured. "Word on the street is that you guys like your brandy," he said, handing first Maze and then Roy a glass. Then he asked Antwon what was he drinking.

"Just water for now."

"Water for now," Bloc said, "and we can talk about the later, later."

Bloc felt negligent and guilty. Negligent because he reasoned he himself, not Roy and Maze, should have been the one to secure Antwon's release. Guilty, because although he'd contributed handsomely to the fund Roy established, he'd conceded to what Tish insisted, that Roy and Maze had the access, the privilege, they should use those advantages and lead the charge to benefit Antwon. It wasn't the conceding that made him feel guilty, though, it was the relief he felt once he had.

Shortly Cynthia and Lavia had the food out and set up and ready for self-serve and they joined the others in the great room. Roy cleared his throat and said he had good news to share. Cynthia noted that Roy and Bloc were in the same turtleneck— Roy's was navy—and she was so caught up in that observation that it took a minute for it to register that he was announcing that all charges against Antwon were being dropped. Cheers went up as they hugged Antwon and patted his back, and Bloc even offered Roy a fist bump though Roy missed on the first two attempts.

"Well, there's never been a higher note on which to proclaim that dinner is served," Tish said, and they gathered around the table shaped like a fried egg with its irregular edges.

"Everything smells delightful," Maze said, as she spooned raspberry dressing over her salad. "And the chicken, ah, do I detect sage?"

"You do indeed," Cynthia said. "The recipe was handed down from my grandmother who never made the acquaintance of a measuring spoon, so I never know whether or not I've got the proportions right."

"Well, Maze insists one can never use too much sage," Roy said, as he put two chicken thighs on his plate. "She spent a year living among the Indigenous people of the Amazon rain forest and their sage rituals were special indeed."

"They most certainly were," Maze chimed from the table as she spread her napkin and waited for the others. "I'd feel both cleansed and insightful after."

"Sounds fascinating," Lavia said. "Maybe you'll lead us all in a sage ritual. What do we need besides sage?"

"For one the sage must be fresh, and it must be properly sourced," Maze said, as she sipped water. "So much has to do with the intention, so I wouldn't recommend using sage purchased from a place where profit, not healing and enlightenment, is the motive."

"Well, that settles that," Cynthia said, as she remembered back to decades ago when Gabriella had waved a burning wand of sage through Cynthia and E's house before they moved in, purifying it. And before that, when Gabriella was still testing her powers, she'd burned sage in Cynthia's dorm room to help her still live in that dorm after that night with Mr. Z. "Where in America is profit not the motive?" she added, to dismiss the image of her dorm.

"Touché," Roy said, as he spooned macaroni and cheese onto his plate.

"And regardless, we don't want to take away from the time we have with Antwon," Tish said, as she joined the others at the table, setting a basket filled with garlic bread in the center.

"Right," added Bloc. "'Cause if I were Anton, right about now I'd be itching to look at my watch to see how much longer I'd have to suffer through with these old people."

They all laughed, and Bloc asked Roy what had happened for the charges to be dropped.

"Well, apparently the prosecutor was handed evidence that disavowed the witness's testimony, so she recanted rather than face perjury charges."

"What evidence?" Tish asked. "Had you all hired a private detective?"

"Not at that point, though the plan was on the table."

"It was likely a weak case, and they knew it," Lavia said. Lavia certainly knew how weak the case was. A white woman claimed to have watched Antwon put a bag over the head of a shop owner as the man was locking up his hair and beauty supply store, and then rob him of the thousands of dollars in cash he carried. The woman had also been the witness in two similar cases in as many years, where she fingered young Black men for robbing owners of beauty supply stores. In those cases the victims had also had their heads covered from behind and could not identify their assailants. That one person witnessed two almost identical crimes should have been a bright red flag, but the prosecutors were hungry for convictions and gobbled up the white woman's story. Had it not been for Lavia's sleuthing that she considered amateur hour, it was so basic, Antwon might have met a similar fate. Lavia performed a simple background check of the principal witness, and learned that the woman was a meth addict who'd been arrested for shoplifting, purse snatching, and drug possession. Each time her dealer—himself arrested but not convicted for robbing the owner of a beauty supply store—put up the money to secure her release.

Lavia penned a report connecting those facts. With Robert's okay, she used the letterhead of Robert's firm and sent the report to both the public defender assigned to Antwon's case, and to the district attorney. She didn't want Antwon to feel beholden. Robert's firm had an international reputation and she imagined that that D.A.'s office was quaking in its boots given how quickly charges were dropped against Antwon, and the two other young men were in the process of seeing their convictions overturned.

"Well, let's not diminish all the behind-the-scenes efforts from Roy and the team he assembled," Tish said.

"Indeed," Lavia said, as she looked at Antwon and he looked embarrassed as he cut into his chicken thigh and Lavia wondered if it was because he felt like a charity case. "But let's also not diminish how racist the criminal justice system is in in the first place that Antwon was even in that horrible situation."

"Amen to that," Maze said.

"I second that emotion, Lavia," from Bloc as he chowed down on his chicken.

"I'm sure Antwon is grateful to Roy and company; what say you, Antwon?" Tish smiled at Antwon.

"You are under no obligation to respond to that, Antwon," Lavia said, biting the ends of her words. "I mean really, what the hell, Tish?"

Tish just sat there, her mouth in the shape of a gasp as the room went silent as snowfall.

"I'm just saying"—Lavia broke the silence—"that I've just returned from Australia where I buried my dad and he spent his life beholden to people who he should have never been beholden to, you know what I mean, to the invaders."

Cynthia and Bloc looked at each other and Bloc mouthed, *Australia*, and Cynthia hunched her shoulders.

"Because what happens is that that bullshit gets internalized by someone like my dad, who was Indigenous Australian."

"But Roy didn't invade anything having to do with Antwon. My goodness, Lavia, he got him released, got the charges dropped," Tish said.

"Might I just say, I'm so sorry about your father," Maze interjected, "about his passing, about the treatment he suffered at the hands of the invaders, especially in his youth."

"Wow, and all this time I thought you were Indian," Roy

said, and Maze turned and looked at him with a how-did-I-marry-such-a-dumb-asshole expression.

"Well, no, I'm not. I'm a descendant of the First Peoples of Australia. I was born on a cruise ship where my parents worked around the clock, the best parents anyone could have. That's who I'm grateful to, not some white man who threw them crumbs."

"Absolutely, that's who you should honor, Lavia," Maze said.

"Let the church say amen," Bloc said, throwing everything he had at the fire erupting between Lavia and Tish.

"It feels good to say that, finally," Lavia said. "My parents both escaped situations forced on them, and they were afraid they would be found out; even when it no longer mattered that my father had run away from a government-sanctioned home, they were still afraid they would suffer consequences if the truth was known. So I held their truth, and also the truth about who I am. No, Roy, I am not Indian, and it feels so good to not have to live with your assumptions anymore."

"Well, Lavia, I'm speechless," Tish said. "I mean, damn, girl, you could have trusted me."

"Back to you, right, Tish. It always comes back to you. You should try what I just did, honor your own dead father. Or is that what you did earlier when you freaked out over a song about a sex worker. Were you taking up for your father? Was that his thing? Prostitutes? I know what killed my father, what killed yours?"

"What the hell are you talking about, Lavia? Are you drunk or high or something?" Tish said.

Lavia closed her eyes and shook her head. She'd overstepped, she knew. The air in the room crackled like a fire in search of kindling to keep itself alive. Nobody spoke. Cynthia tried to process what was happening. What was Lavia implying about Tish's father, that he frequented whorehouses? She stood up then, her hand to her head. The room had tilted suddenly. Was Lavia saying that Tish's father had been killed by a prostitute? The thought made her dizzy. No, not the thought. Vertigo. She knew this was an attack of vertigo coming on. She hadn't had an attack since she'd moved here.

"I've got to go," she said. "I've got this silly dizziness thing that's threatening to show itself."

"Oh no, sister girl," Tish said. "What is it? You know you're welcome to go stretch out in my guest room." Her voice shook.

"Thanks, Tish," Cynthia said. "But I've got medicine at home, and my own bed is calling out to me so I'm gonna heed that call and head on in."

Bloc stood, concern swathing his face. "I'll walk home with you," he offered, surprising Cynthia.

"No, no, no, somebody's got to referee this sibling rivalry," she said. "A few more shouts of 'Let the church say amen' should do it."

They all laughed; even Antwon, who'd been like a wooden soldier to this point in the meal, laughed. Tish blew Cynthia a kiss, Lavia gave her a thumbs-up, she nestled herself in her cashmere wrap and was out the door.

Thirteen

Cynthia was leaned back in her orange corduroy swivel chair, swaddled under a quilt, her feet propped on the matching ottoman. The dizziness had subsided and right now she took sips of water and pressed against the worn soft corduroy thinking about everything and nothing in particular, just a jumble of thoughts piled high that included her uneaten sage chicken at Tish's horrid, irregularly shaped dining table. She resisted thinking about whatever was going on between Lavia and Tish; that hurt to think about. She especially resisted considering what Lavia had said about Tish's father. Now she was watching the explosion of light from the motion sensor on her patio, and Bloc's frame appeared as if the light had created him. She still jumped when she heard the doorbell chime even as she saw him standing there.

She hit the toggle that flashed on her phone, releasing the front lock on the door, and watched Bloc walk in, tentatively, as if he was unsure whether she meant to open the door or not.

"Hey, Miss Lady, I just wanted to make sure you were okay."

"Miss Lady? I thought that was your name of endearment for Tish," Cynthia said matter-of-factly without condemnation.

"I don't really have a name of endearment for Tish," he said, as he walked all the way into the dimly lit room and took in the wall of framed photos of Cynthia's son from infancy to his wedding day, the mile-high shelves crowded with books, the olive-toned velvet couch with matching wing chairs of gold and green. Such rich, deep colors, so opposite from the breeziness, the lightness that was Tish's house. "All settled in, I see; place has changed since I was last here," he said.

"I've changed since you were last here," she replied, as she nestled deeper in her chair and pulled the quilt up to her chin.

"Yeah? Not too much, I hope, I really liked you as you were."

"So much so you just blotted me on out as if . . . as if . . . whatever. It doesn't matter now."

"It does matter, Cynthia. It really does. Honest to God. It's just that Tish and I, uh, I don't know, even now I can't say what Tish and I are, but you know, it was so awkward that first time we were all together at Tish's and I wanted to, you know, talk to you at some point after. And just explain, and apologize, and . . . Damn. I'm sorry. I'm just plain and simply sorry."

Cynthia hunched her shoulders. "I'm over it. Not that it was much to get over."

"Ouch, that was cold," he said, shifting his weight from one foot to the other. "Can you at least offer a hurt brother a seat after stomping on my ego like that?"

"Damn, the fact that I opened the door and let you in should be enough. Now I got to offer you a seat? You want me to bake you a pie, too?"

"Uh, lemon?" he asked, sheepishly.

She didn't answer, didn't laugh, or sigh, or curse so he just stood there.

"So did Tish and Lavia work through whatever they had to work through? I mean, that was some heavy shit going on between the two of them. All in front of white people, too. I feel so sad, they're otherwise so close."

"Let me just say it got worse before it got better," Bloc said, taking her question as permission to sit, which he did, albeit stiffly, on the edge of the couch. The couch, though, was so pliable that it pulled him all the way in, nestling him, and he almost sighed at how good sitting on this couch felt, as he told Cynthia that initially Lavia apologized, said that maybe she had had too much wine. "We settled in and, you know, were enjoying the meal, which I was happy about because it seemed rude to otherwise be smacking my lips over that sage chicken while they were battling each other like Spartan warriors. But then Tish revisited the whole fawning over Roy, and how much the legal team he'd assembled had done. And Roy lapped up the praise and said they had filed this and that motion and Lavia said that she was sure that Maze would have done at least that in her role as a public defender earning not much more than a preschool teacher. So they went back and forth, Lavia practically called Roy a dumbass, said Tish was being disingenuous, 'cause she thought the dinner was about Antwon, not about Roy. And what can I say, a couple of 'fuck you bitches' got thrown back and forth."

"No, no, no," Cynthia moaned, her hand to her head.

"It got better, though, after the sage burning."

"Really? Y'all really did the sage thing?"

"We really did," Bloc said. "Of all people, poor Antwon saved the night. He made a joke by remarking that maybe that sage ritual wasn't such a bad idea after all. And Maze jumped all on the idea. She and Roy had sat beet red and silent once the argument really got going. So Maze hurriedly took those sage leaves that you had adorning the chicken platter, and used a chicken bone from Roy's plate as a wand, and wrapped the sage around the bone and stuck it in the candle flame."

"Wha?" Cynthia said, her mouth hanging.

"For real. She asked everybody to close their eyes and inhale and think of peace and harmony, as she waved the chicken bone around, and then she led us in a chant."

"You are telling a lie," Cynthia said, laughing as she imagined it. "Y'all did not chant to a chicken bone."

"Believe me, we did. And it was damn sure calming Tish and Lavia, who both had their eyes pressed shut; they started crying as we held hands and I saw them squeezing each other's hands. I felt for Antwon, though; he was sitting there trying to be polite, but couldn't do a thing with the what-the-fuck-situation-am-I-caught-up-in-with-these-old-ass-weird-ass-people expression plastered to his face."

"Damn," Cynthia said, tossing her quilt and swinging her legs around and off the ottoman.

"Well, yeah, as I'm telling you about it now, that was some funny shit. But for me in the moment, I was really praying that it would do something to help Lavia and Tish."

"And it did, please tell me that it did."

"Like magic, it seems, they were back to themselves, you

know, a little stilted, but listening and nodding when the other spoke. They even laughed at some private joke while they made coffee together."

"Well, I'm happy to hear that. What was going on with them?" Cynthia asked the air in her cottage as much as she asked Bloc. "Is it that Lavia's especially sensitive right now because her grief is so raw? You know, she's exposed and tender and grappling with the secret she's kept all these years."

"I'm sure that's it. But what about Tish? Why is Tish so pro-fucking Roy?" Bloc said, and then stopped when he realized how that sounded.

"You said it, not me," Cynthia gasped.

"No, no, no." Bloc sat forward and waved his hands around. "I meant the f-word as an adjective, not the verb form. I was describing Roy, not saying, you know what I mean." He gave up trying to explain himself.

"Oh, okaaay," Cynthia said, drawing out the okay. "You got to watch those dangling participles. Maybe that's what Tish and Lavia were giggling about, Roy's dangling participle. You know Tish will go there."

Bloc looked away, his profile stoic, his jaw clenched.

"I'm sorry, that was unkind of me," she said.

He reached into his jacket pocket then and pulled out two fat marijuana cigarettes. "You can make it up to me and help me out with these."

"Damn," she said, as she went to the couch and sat next to him. "I haven't seen stogies like those since the seventies."

"Trust me, you didn't smoke stogies like these in the seventies," he said as he twirled the marijuana-stuffed cigarettes between his fingers. "The THC is triple what it was back then. In fact, you'll have to turn your exhaust on full power or your neighbors might get a contact high."

Cynthia laughed. "I don't even own an ashtray anymore."

"You have an old saucer?"

"I do."

"We could smoke over the counter, let our ash fall in the saucer. You can hit your exhaust—" Bloc said, as he began pulling himself up from the couch, remarking that this couch was so hard to leave.

"Well, sit there," Cynthia said, already in the kitchen. "I've got a chipped saucer perfect for an ashtray. What would you like to drink? Offerings are more substantial than they were the last time you were here."

"Offerings last time were the best I've had," he said, intending to whisper that to himself, then tried to call it back when he realized his whisper had floated easily on the air and followed Cynthia into the kitchen area. "I'm sorry, I was out of line with that," he said.

"Are you ever in line?" she asked, back in the great room, standing over him, handing him the saucer, then leaning to click on the lamp atop the end table next to where he sat.

The lampshade was a brocaded swirl of olive and gold and cast a light the color of autumn. She picked up Bloc's face through the green and gold light and wondered what expression he saw on hers as his face fell in on itself, as if he was suddenly so weakened by the sight of her that the muscles in his face just gave up, just collapsed in the autumn light. She wondered if she'd just given him the look that she'd been ready to flash when Tish suddenly turned off "Lady Marmalade" right before Patti preened in French, *Do you want to sleep with me tonight?* Cynthia wondered if it was the look she'd see her mother flash right before a man's face did as Bloc's was doing now. Wondered if it was the look she gave Mr. Z that night.

"What do you see?" she asked him then.

"What? What do you mean?" Bloc asked, trying to shake his face to normal.

"My face. What do you see on my face?"

"Is this a trick question?" He forced a laugh.

"No, I'm serious. Is my face looking like I'm coming on to you? I really need to know, 'cause I had a situation, I mean years ago, when someone told me that. He said everything about my face signaled that I wanted to be with him. And it's been really, really plaguing me lately. And right now, it's like everything about you is responding to me as if I'm coming on to you."

"Well, damn, I mean, I don't know, do you want me to think you're coming on to me? I'm happy to think that if that's what you want. Is that what you want, Cynthia?"

"Answer my question first."

"Your question? I mean, I don't know if this, what would I call it, desire? Is that what you mean? I think that's what you mean, right? Are you asking me who's initiating it? I don't know, to be completely honest. How about we figure it all out over a little weed?"

"No, how about before a little weed," Cynthia said, as she scooted the ottoman over and sat in front of him.

Her eyes with the odd mix of severity and kindness bombarded Bloc. He felt shaken, but also strangely softened by the way the gold and green light held steady between them, making it easier for him to not look away. He sat up and leaned forward toward Cynthia and tried to explain.

. . .

Bloc was seeing his mother's eyes as he looked at Cynthia. Her stare weakened him down to his essential truth the same way his mother's had. At that moment with Cynthia he was showing what he wanted. He wanted Cynthia, not Tish. That had been true for him the moment he saw Cynthia at the reception though he'd worked hard not to acknowledge it.

And that day when he looked at his mother, he was also telling on himself because his mother's face was impossible to lie to.

He was ten minutes late that day. Arrived at Scotty's Hoagie and Variety at 4:17 instead of 4:07. His mother had already moved from the counter stool where she was usually seated when he walked into Scotty's and was standing at the door. Her barrel-shaped bang sat higher along her forehead and he could see the vertical crease in her forehead and he wondered how long the crease had held. Generally, it was a fleeting interruption of the smoothness of her skin, like when they were out and she'd look up and the sky was gray and she'd note that it might rain and she didn't have her umbrella and the line would appear, but just as quickly it would fade and her beautiful forehead would return to its perfect coffee-with-cream brown. Today, though, the line held as she asked him what happened to him, and he stammered, "Nothing."

"Were you fighting?"

"No, no," he said, as if that was the worst thing he could do.

"Your lip looks red," she said. "Why is your lip red?"

"Must've bit it when I was eating red licorice."

"Red licorice, huh?" she said, as they walked out of Scotty's and Scotty shouted, "Don't worry, Maryann, I got him. Tomorrow we start working on that left hook, all right, Bloc?"

Bloc laughed and gave Scotty a thumbs-up. His mother didn't laugh; that line held on her forehead the whole three-block walk home.

It seemed to deepen as Bloc sat at the kitchen table and did his homework while she cooked. No humming now or chattering the way she usually did as she cooked, laughing as she recalled some funny thing that happened at Scotty's during the day. She turned from the stove to look at him each time she added a new ingredient to the ground beef she browned, as she stirred in the green peppers, the onions, the garlic. By the time she rifled through the drawer for the can opener to separate the lids from tins of tomato paste, he thought his chest would explode. He announced that he was done his homework and asked if he could go outside for fifteen minutes before dinner.

"I'm not letting you go outside," she said. "I'm not letting you go anywhere till you tell me why you were a full ten minutes late getting to Scotty's with a busted lip."

"My lip's not busted," he said, as he ran his tongue over his lip. "I told you it's from the licorice."

"And the licorice made you late? Where'd you get the licorice?"

"From Turtle." He tried to put a laugh to his voice as he said, "Come on, Mom, you know fat and slow Turtle always has his pockets stuffed with candy."

His mother didn't laugh the way she usually did when he joked about his friends, even as she'd remind him that the jokes were just between them because it was not kind to tease people because they were fat or slow. She poured the boiled spaghetti in a colander in the sink. She put a plate on top of the cast-iron skillet where the tomato paste erupted through the meat like miniature volcanoes. She turned the stove off and sat right in front of him. He wished the phone would ring the way it sometimes did when she cooked and it would be his grandmother, or one of his aunts, or a choir member, or a PTA member and his mother would make good use of the extralong cord she'd had installed on the wall phone in the kitchen. She could hold the phone to her ear and move all around the kitchen from the fridge to the cabinets as she chopped and stirred and poured. "Girl, hush" was the refrain followed by the music that was her laughter, perfect background sounds for Bloc as he figured out the math problems that were three chapters ahead of the rest of the class.

The phone was woefully silent, though, as he watched his mother move her face closer to his, so close that he felt his glasses fogging from her breath; so close that the line on her forehead grew so deep, so long, that it seemed to move all the way to her chin, seemed to slice her face in two. Her voice rose up then. It was like the voice of God in *The Ten Commandments* movie. "Tell me what happened," the voice said, said it slowly, deeply. And he began to cry.

. . .

Bloc managed not to cry as he sat on Cynthia's couch and told her that she brought out a certain honesty in him. "I guess my face just goes naked when I look at you sometimes. You know, I'm innocent again. I'm ten years old and sitting at the kitchen table doing my homework while my mother made spaghetti; and she's asking me why I'm late getting to the store where she worked, because I was never late. And I'm praying that she doesn't look at me because my face will tell on me, and she'll know I'm trying to keep a secret. And it did. She demanded to know about the very thing that I needed to keep secret. You bring out that same apprehension that, you know, with you it's all about the truth and nothing but. I don't know if it's your eyes . . . actually, it *is* your eyes."

"So is this a good thing or bad thing that I remind you of your mother in this moment?" Cynthia asked.

"Oh," he said with a cough. "I mean definitely a good thing in that you make me want to reach down and pull up the better version of myself, and I know it might seem weird in this context when we're talking about, you know, whether I thought you were coming on to me, for me to start spouting off about how you remind me of my mother. I promise you there was nothing freaky about my relationship with my mother, you know, she was my first love like every mother is her son's first love. I guess the gist of what I'm saying, admittedly muddled though it may be, is that you and she share that quality that makes it impossible for me to lie. So no, to answer your question, I didn't sense that you were necessarily coming on to me. But when you leaned down to click on that light, and you were caught up in the golden hue, I was, like, damn, I want this woman so bad. It was just an honest thought, a pure thought, and it showed, that's all. My face told on me."

Cynthia looked up at the ceiling where the blue-black night pulsed through the skylight. "So it wasn't me," she said. "I wasn't sending you signals that, you know—" Her voice dropped off as she looked at Bloc again, and then beyond him.

"No, pretty lady, it was not." Bloc stilled the impulse to rub his hands up and down her arms. "So whatever's plaguing you about something some joker told you years ago, well, I don't know about then. I only know about now. Only tonight."

"Only tonight," she said, trying to orient herself to the here and now because she felt herself tumbling back to the night in her dorm room with Mr. Z. She was seeing his hands curved around her feet, which he'd put in his lap. Her heels rubbed against his wide-wale corduroy pants and the sensation was so rapturous it was unbearable as he massaged her feet. He manipulated the bones and tendons, manipulated her logic, her emotions, even the words coming out of her mouth, squeezing her words to make them mean what she had not at all meant. She closed her eyes, trying not to see him, but there was his smile that tilted more to one side, the hint of gray in his mustache that was so precisely cut, it could have been painted on. He was looking at her feet as if they were the most beautiful things, the same way he'd looked at her when she caught his eye from where she sat front and center at Irvine Auditorium.

"Earth to Cynthia," Bloc said, pulling her back, saving her from the whole of the recollection.

She shook her head to focus her eyes. "Sorry, I was just thinking about what you said." She reached for one of the stogies patient on the end table. "Why don't you perform a public service and help a sister get her loose turned on and fire up this fat-ass joint."

They got really high then. Stupid high. Laughing uncontrollably at nothing high. They devoured a peach cobbler Cynthia had bought the day before at the farmers' market, causing Bloc to exclaim, "I'm in fucking heaven." Which led to a dissertation on whether there would be sex in heaven. Bloc said absolutely 'cause it's, well, heaven. Cynthia thought that the heaven joy would be more complete than the satisfaction that comes from sex. "You know, a sexual climax ends 'cause it's not sustainable. I think in heaven, it's sustainable."

"Well, let me get my house in order then," Bloc said. "'Cause I want to spend eternity in a state of sustainable sexual climax."

"You do know that's blasphemous, right?" Cynthia said.

"No, sitting this close to you with my hands to myself is blasphemous."

"Well, damn, Negro," she said. "Don't be no blasphemer."

• • •

The rising sun leaned in to the skylight to peek at Cynthia and Bloc wrapped up in each other on the couch, snoring soundly. The sun turned shy at what she saw and motioned a cloud over to curtain them, half dressed as they were from their waists down. Cynthia was on top of Bloc, the tail of her blouse dipping just low enough to barely cover her behind, though her thighs were fully exposed. As shapely as they were, her thighs were also huge; more than huge, they were gigantic. So large that the cloud even drifted back, giving a trio of blackbirds a view, causing them to crow out a collective daaaamn.

The sounds of the birds flapping and tweeting over the skylight woke Cynthia. She jerked up, taking seconds to realize where she was, who she was with. Then she lay back down and positioned her head over Bloc's chest; she needed the rhythm of its rise and fall. She pushed herself over so that she was no longer straddling him, then rolled off the couch. She picked their clothes off the floor. Thought about covering herself in case he woke before she got to the bedroom. Then said what the hell. Her body was what it was, and really she wasn't in terrible shape. Except for thighs that she'd always thought defied nature given that her arms, her shoulders, her chest were small in comparison. Though she'd come to appreciate their girth since she'd become a sexagenarian and learned that cellulite-expanded thighs actually had a medical benefit because they trapped fat that would otherwise be traveling through her body finding arteries to clog. She'd called Gabriella when she read the piece. Managed to say through her hysterical laughter, *Gab, science has weighed in, and my fat-ass thighs are keeping me alive.* Cynthia smiled to herself as she folded Bloc's pants over the back of her orange chair. Even his phone had landed on the floor and she set it on the end table. She took her time walking to the bedroom. He'd certainly had no problem with her thighs as he'd uttered *Lawd, lawd, lawd* when he'd moved between them.

Bloc was up and sitting at the counter when Cynthia returned to the great room. She'd showered and dressed and felt bright and light and loose in a yellow open-weave sweater and orange stretchy ankle pants.

"Whoa, be still my heart," he said. "You are one beautiful daybreak."

She smiled and thought about giving him a good morning kiss, but decided against. "Coffee?" she asked instead, as she went straight to the stove and ran water in the teakettle and set it on the stove and turned on the flame. "I do a pretty banging French press if I do say so myself. I've got yogurt and strawberries that I usually mix with Cheerios in place of granola if you'd also like."

"I'd also like," he said over the sound of coffee beans being crushed in the grinder.

"So I was wondering," she said, pausing to count how many tablespoons of coffee she dropped into the carafe. "Why were you late?"

He answered with raised eyebrows. "When was I late?"

"Last night when you said I bring out an honesty in you like your mom used to, and you mentioned the time that you were terrified because you were late meeting your mother and she could see on your face that it was some big secret. I was just wondering why were you late? What was your secret? Did your mom ever wrangle it out of you?"

"Oh boy, did she ever," he said. "But before I get into that, I gotta see a man about a horse, and if you could point me toward a shower, a towel, and a bar of soap, I'll be in your debt."

Once in the bathroom he texted Tish to tell her he'd have to miss the breakfast she'd planned for today with her cousin and her cousin's grandchild. He didn't know which would disappoint Tish more, that Tish would miss his company, or that she would miss the opportunity to show off her little cousin.

He felt a line of reflux move up his throat as he showered and thought about the fallout once he told Tish that he wanted to be with Cynthia now. Thought about the pain of severing his relationship with Tish that really had a solid friendship as its foundation. Thought about Lavia. He had such huge affection for Lavia, and he'd be putting her in the position of having to take sides. He'd also be responsible for casting Cynthia as a conniving man stealer.

He turned the water hotter as he lathered up with Cynthia's soap that smelled of lavender and mint. Was *man stealer* even a term? he wondered. Was he making himself out to be more than he was? Tish might toss her hands and say, *Whatever, y'all still welcome here for our regular get-togethers long as she brings food and you bring weed.*

The thought humored him and he laughed as he rinsed down and stayed in the shower long after he was finished. The hot water pelleted his skin. He inhaled the lavender-scented steam. He thought about the looming conversation with Cynthia about the secret he'd tried to keep from his mother over being ten minutes late. His body shook convulsively and he realized he'd begun to cry.

Cynthia sipped her coffee on the back patio while Bloc was in the shower. It was unseasonably warm for January—60 degrees and rising according to the forecast. A breeze stirred and rippled the fringes of the yellow awning that preened over her patio. The sweater she wore and the awning were perfect matches, complemented by the woven orange placemats and the coffee mugs that were swirls of orange and yellow. She thought back to the first time she'd gone to Tish's house and noted how everything about Tish matched everything about her decor down to her nail polish and the linen napkins. She'd wondered what that said about Tish, that she would plan the colors to the minutest details. She now wondered if Tish's matched colors had been a coincidence, like Cynthia's yellow sweater matching the awning was a coincidence. Or had she herself planned it all out as she dressed this morning, unaware that a deeper part of her directed her moves? Had her eye gone to the window and caught the yellow of the awning as she rifled through her closet? Had she gotten a glimpse of herself sitting under the awning, sipping coffee, the preponderance of yellow highlighting the undertones of her brown skin? Had she planned out that night with Mr. Z as she'd swathed her skin with cocoa butter and put on her lacy bikini panties and the ribbed semiopaque undershirt that highlighted her nipples? Was she a worse version of her mother? Divine at least externalized her intentions, wore her intentions like the belts she'd wrap around her tiny waist to accentuate the side-to-side motion of her slim hips.

She stopped her thinking as she watched Bloc step onto the patio. Something had broken inside him—she could tell by his reddened eyes that showed through his glasses even though they weren't nonreflective lenses. More than his eyes, though, it was the air around him that had a bruised feel, as if he'd just been trying to punch through the air because that thing that had broken inside him needed a place to go so he had to make a hole in the air that was large enough to suck up that thing, to exhume it, once and for all. She understood that need. "Are you okay?" she asked softly, matching the breeze that drifted back and forth under the awning.

He forced a smile. "Why wouldn't I be?" he said. "Out here on this beautiful patio on this beautiful day with a beautiful woman."

"You seem—" She fell silent then. Reversed herself from diagnosing his mood, from telling him what she thought about how he seemed. It did not matter what she thought right now. She poured coffee into the mug she'd set out for him. Asked him how he took his coffee.

"Cream, no sugar," he said as he sighed and pulled back the chair and sat down across from her. Bloc realized how different Cynthia was from Tish. Tish would not have wondered about a conversation they'd had the night before. Would not have sensed that the snippet about his mother was related to some larger thing and remembered to ask him about it.

Ten minutes, that's all, he'd only been ten minutes late getting to Scotty's store that day, he told Cynthia now. That short space of time that was like a millennium. He'd lost his footing and fell as he ran through Rochester's living room, the way he ran through Rochester's living room every day, zigzagging to make it harder for Rochester to get close enough to swipe his fingers against Bloc, fingers that Bloc thought looked like the last french fries in the bottom of the bag, fat and soggy, the ones that would make him want to vomit. Bloc landed against the coffee table when he fell. He hit his mouth. He sucked his lip to swallow his blood even as he struggled to get away from Rochester, who took advantage of the fall and pounced like a jackal that isn't animal enough to kill its own prey, that waits for the lion to do the hard work to take the zebra down, then comes in like the winnowing cowardly thief that it is, stealing away a little boy's innocence. Bloc managed to crawl to the dining room even though Rochester clutched his legs. He propelled himself until he was under the mammoth dining room pedestal table. He could hear Shelly's shrieks coming from the basement below. Usually he'd already fought Rochester off by then and had gotten to the basement door and opened the door and watched Shelly fly up those steps as if she had wings, as if she was the angel that Bloc knew her to be. Surely Shelly must know that too much time had passed for Bloc to reach her.

"Do you think Shelly knew?" he had asked his mother as he broke down at the kitchen table and told her what had happened in those ten minutes. "Shelly didn't run up the basement steps like she usually did. I had to go all the way down to her. And when I got to the bottom step I saw that she already pooped on the basement floor. She looked at me like she was ashamed of herself. Then she came to me and licked my face and cried. I never heard her cry before and I think she cried because she knew and that made me saddest of all." He described for Cynthia how comforting the kitchen smells were as he unburdened himself to his mother; the onions and garlic, the green pepper, the spaghetti patient in the colander in the sink, steam still rising. His mother's eyes were a comfort, too, as they grew round as buttons, unblinking.

Right now he watched Cynthia's eyes go large as he told her what happened, told her from the perspective of sitting in his mother's kitchen. It made the telling easier because he could describe how his mother grabbed him to her so tightly and swayed him so gently and how soothing her sway was. Told her that they sat like that for half the night; he fell asleep against his mother's chest, and when he woke, his mother told him not to linger on what happened under that monster's dining room table, told him to linger instead on the fact that his momma loves him more than life. Then she rocked him like he was a newborn, and that brought him peace.

When he was finished, he sipped coffee from the yellow and orange swirled cup under the yellow awning. He felt lighter now; the air around him, too, had a floaty quality, as if layers had been removed, as if his fever had broken and the chills were gone and one by one the blankets could come off.

"Motherfucker." Cynthia spit the word through her teeth. "Fucking pedophile demon motherfucker."

"I'm sorry," Bloc said, "that's some heavy shit to lay on you first thing in the morning like this. We should be reading the paper and cursing about asshole Trump; at least we can channel that anger, we can donate to our candidates and go to downtown Philly and demonstrate with the Indivisibles, and make phone calls and do our get out the vote planning." He put energy under his words. Hoping that his words would have enough power to swat down the question he knew was coming next. His words did not.

"What happened to him?" she asked. "Did your mother, you know, contact the police?"

"She did not, would not, she knew that I would suffer more than he did should it be public record."

"And him?"

It was only a question, the most logical question given the unburdening he'd just done. He looked up. The yellow awning was suddenly too bright, blinding him like the whiteness from a cop's strobe light pointing in his face. "He died."

"Died? When? How? Did he ever have to pay for what he did to you?"

"I assume he's still burning in hell right now."

"But on earth?"

"You know, who can say?"

"How long after did he die?"

"Not very long at all."

"Well, good. That's good to know. Good."

Bloc nodded as he sipped his coffee. He could have told her now how Rochester died the next day, gutted with the same type of switchblade Scotty had given him. He could have described for her how he'd made his way to the corner of Rochester's block fingering the switchblade, having already made his plan. But the block was already barricaded when he turned the corner with what seemed like a thousand police cars; beyond them a crowd had formed. He heard his mother calling out to him from the crowd. "Looks like somebody broke in his house, messed him up real bad. He might not make it," she said, concern swathing her face, and Bloc knew that it was concern not for Rochester, but for him. He could have told Cynthia how he started to cry, worrying about Shelly, and his mother told him that Scotty had Shelly, that Shelly was waiting outside the store as if she knew Bloc would be there. And then when he rushed to the store he was so excited to see Shelly, tail wagging, that he barely noticed that Scotty's arm was in a homemade sling, his hand wrapped with bags of frozen peas, and Scotty said that damnedest thing, he'd messed up his shoulder back in the storage room trying to get to the carton of bright pink sponge hair rollers 'cause they were hot sellers these days.

No need to tell Cynthia that now, he thought. It was morning still, morning over this patio, morning between them, there was time to fill in the details. Right now he'd enjoy the feel of the sun.

Fourteen

Cynthia walked around with Bloc's story in her head the entire day. Beyond vacillating between feelings of sadness for Bloc, and an anger for Rochester that was so large it would shorten her breath and she'd have to remind herself to stop and be present so that her chest could open again, she also thought about Bloc's mother. Measured Maryann's actions against what Divine's had been in the immediate aftermath of the horribleness of that night Cynthia experienced with Mr. Z.

She'd actually seen Divine the day after. Gabriella had urged her to and even quoted her preacher uncle's advice that the first thing you should do when something bad happens to you is the next thing you had planned to do before it happened. So Cynthia walked from her high-rise campus apartment to her grandmother's house, because that had been her plan the day before. She stopped at the deli on Spruce Street to get a loaf of pumpernickel bread, and a half pound of sweet butter. The store was alive with the smells of dill pickles and cabbage soup and whitefish. The chatter and the laughter were loud, as were the visuals, cases loaded with sides of beef and rounds of liverwurst and mounds of cheeses ready for slicing. The old man who'd cut her butter from the massive yellow brick interrupted his Sinatra imitation to smile at her and ask her how far did she have to go, did she need some ice in the bag to keep the butter chilled. She nodded, robotically; she was still numb with shock. "Ah, look at this beauty," he said as he held up a loaf of bread as if it were Olympic gold. "Just baked, still hot. I wrap it separate from the butter. You hold it close, better it melt your heart than the butter." She tried to smile in response, but the muscles in her face weren't working right now, shut down, it seemed to her, because they just needed a break.

She held both bags close to her as she walked the remaining mile to Rose's. She needed the extremes to jump-start her emotional thermostat that had died the way a car battery dies after the headlights have been on all night. She needed the blend of aromas, too, the righteousness of the warm bread, the innocence of the butter, could she ever claim either again.

The trees on her grandmother's block had begun their late October twirl. The colors floating through the air used to excite her from as long ago as she could remember. She and her grandmother made up a game they called red yellow orange gold when they'd count the leaves as they fell and try to predict which color would win. For years after, every autumn she'd revive the game in her head when she walked through this narrow block of tidy row houses charmed from end to end with trees. This day the falling leaves were not a reminder of simple pleasures with her grandmom; the scene instead filled her with the dark thought that when something is most beautiful, it has already begun to die. Even that dismal idea did nothing to interrupt the flat line that was her emotional state, to at least make it dip into sadness, to at least make her feel.

But then she stepped into her grandmother's vestibule listening for the familiar buzz of the television, the white people's sanitized voices spouting their lines, her grandmother talking back to them, calling them heifers and cows and cackling hens, boars and horses' asses. Instead she heard her mother's laughter, followed by, "Mom, you a mess."

Her mother's laughter, here in her grandmother's living room! The shock of it nicked away at the numbness that had been with Cynthia since the middle of the night; with her as she moved zombielike through her classes; with her on the walk to her grandmother's house through the wildness that was mostly the white periphery of campus until she crossed over to the more settled-in blacker version of West Philly with its hair salons and churches and swept porches that looked over hedges below. Her mother rarely came to Rose's, and when she did, it was not to laugh. It was to maybe talk Cynthia home, telling her she'd made her a special treat for dinner. It was to hear her grandmother retort, *How the chile supposed to want to come home, when you living like you living?* It was for Divine to sit and sigh and tell Rose that she was trying, she really was, but it was harder for her because she just wasn't made up like most people. Rose would soften and try to encourage her then, try to talk her into joining church, try to talk her into seeing a doctor, try to talk her into meeting a nice young man, the staying kind. Divine would nod, agree, she'd sit next to Rose and put her head on her shoulder and exhale long and slow. But laugh? She never laughed, not here in her grandmother's living room where sunlight was not the enemy. The medication, the therapy, they must be working, finally, working.

Cynthia pushed through the vestibule into the living room. Both Divine and Rose looked up in slow motion, it seemed, both their mouths pulled back in similar gushy smiles that showed their gums. Both simultaneously exclaimed, "Cynthia!"

"Oh my god, do I smell fresh bread?" Divine said.

"You know it," Rose said. "And you can bet it's pumpernickel."

"And would that be butter in the other bag?" Divine asked.

"Sweet, lightly salted, the best butter made even better 'cause of who just walked through the door carrying it," Rose answered.

Her mother and grandmother were like two cross-country runners jogging in sync, each matching the other's moves. They even lifted their arms at the exact same second for Cynthia to fall into. But then Divine quickened her pace. Her smile vanished, her eyes squinted, her arms lowered. Divine jumped out in front of Rose, stepping, stepping faster still, to get to Cynthia. Cynthia felt each step in her chest, as if her mother's graceful fingers were pulling against the flatness inside her, not the ferocious way she'd pull against the wall in the middle of the night to claim a glistening chunk of plaster. This pull was more like strumming. As if Cynthia's flatlined emotions were strings on a delicate violin brought to life by an unexpected maestro. By Mommy. "Tell Mommy," Divine said, as she rubbed her hands up and down Cynthia's arms and Cynthia could feel the warmth of them even through her peacoat. "Something's happened to you. Tell Mommy what it is. Whatever it is, you can tell me. Tell me. Tell Mommy, please."

Cynthia never could tell Divine. Divine would fault herself, and Cynthia was protective of her mother. Plus, Cynthia faulted Divine enough for the both of them, which caused the guilt to rush up like foul-smelling air rising from a steam vent. Cynthia knew how to hold her breath until she was on the other side of the grate so that the air didn't choke her. Her mother was just learning how to walk adult steps, how to keep moving through the steam even if she couldn't see exactly the path ahead; she was just discovering the benefits of monitoring her moods and making phone calls to her therapist, to members of her support group. That her mother was so committed to her recovery made Cynthia very proud, and strengthened her resolve that Divine need never know.

Fifteen

The March weather had been as erratic as a crazy boss. Sweet and accommodating one day at seventy degrees with a light breeze. All-over-the-place slushy the next. Stone-cold ice storm two days later, beautiful but treacherous. Tish had been like the weather. Warm and inviting one week, hosting a party of a dozen or more of the Gen's residents and basking in their compliments about the way her cottage was decorated, the catered food, the art, the music flowing, the wines she chose. Mostly though, she reveled in the compliments of how good she looked. Even when they didn't say it out loud, she could see it in their eyes. She needed that most of all to protect her from the surge of feelings trying to be acknowledged.

Except her preoccupation with the compliments she received wasn't working like it had most of her adult life, and her mood plummeted to the point where she wasn't hosting, or partying, or being the Gen's vivacious butterfly at a welcome brunch, or karaoke, or samba dance night. She culled her social circle down to just Lavia. They streamed television series and made predictions about whether Issa Rae and Lawrence would get back together on *Insecure*; debated who was the badder ass on *Queen Sugar* between Charley, Nova, and Aunt Vi; and cried like babies when Randall's birth father died on *This Is Us*.

Tish insisted to Lavia that her not wanting to be around people had nothing to do with Bloc asking for a reset on their relationship. He said that he loved her, he really loved her, just not in the way she deserved; he loved her as a friend and he hoped they could be friends, really and truly he did. She'd asked Bloc if Cynthia had anything to do with it, and he replied that he was trying like hell to be an honest man so yeah, she did, yeah.

"Well, if you feel the need to be all partnered up, you could always take a cruise. You know I can tell you all about cruise ships and how to get a date."

"Speaking of cruise ships, Lavia—"

"I'm sorry, too, Tish," Lavia said.

"You're not even gonna let me say it."

"Your face says it."

"Well, I need to say it out of my mouth. I'm so sorry for assuming things about you that I shouldn't have. For focusing so much on myself, you know. If I were a better friend, you know, you could have trusted me more to tell me about your parents. Do you forgive me?"

"I will, if you forgive me for taking my grief out on you. And further, it was on me to clarify who I am, where I'm from, and I chose not to. I mean, I'm okay with that choice, but you don't have to own that part of it. Please don't own that part of it, Tish."

"Well, I'm glad we got that out of the way because you know I don't like to get all mushy," Tish said, even as she teared up.

"Tell me about it. That's one thing we have in common."

"Thank god it's the only thing—"

"Right, I mean who'd want to be all tall and beautiful and gregarious like you, Tish—"

"And who'd want to be all smart and discerning and quick-witted like you, Lavia."

"And who'd want your eye for coordinating a room."

"Well, who'd want your ability to be so honest. Wait, I would. I really would, Lavia." Tish turned serious then. "I wish I had in me to do what you did that night at dinner. I wish I could just announce to a roomful of people, you know, that I'm not who people assumed I was, you know, to reclaim the me that I buried because of my father— I'm just saying I wish I could do that."

"So what's stopping you? You don't have to do it in front of a roomful of people, you could do it right here, with only me."

"I can't—"

"When I told y'all about my parents you said you wished I had trusted you—"

"Yeah, and you rightly pointed out that I was making it about me—"

"So now it *is* about you, Tish."

"I feel like you already know." Tish's voice shook.

"This is not about what I know, okay?"

"Okay," Tish said, pausing to take a deep breath as if she were jumping into nine feet of water for the first time. "So I lied about, you know, about my name, where I'm from, I'm really from New Jersey."

"Shit, who wouldn't lie about that," Lavia said, causing Tish

185

to laugh and then cry, then she was laughing and crying at the same time. Then she just cried as she told Lavia how her father was a social scientist with provocative views. "You know he published a lot of books and was always going to signings and getting back late. So this one night, he went to do a talk, and then just like that, he didn't come back. He just died. Died at a whorehouse. And after he died like that, I was, like, fuck you, man, you're a liar and a fraud. And I intentionally went against everything he said, you know, with intention. I've spent the years since he died working so hard at being the type of person he never wanted me to be. You know, he never wanted me to be all superficial and caught up in my looks. But I thought he was, you know, great, and then I realized he wasn't."

"Well, couldn't he be both, Tish?" Lavia asked as gently as she could. "Couldn't he be a good father and, as you call him, a fraud? Even though, you know, procuring the services of a sex worker is not necessarily fraudulent."

"I know," Tish said, between her sobs. "I'm starting to accept that, and it hurts. I don't hate him. I never did hate him. And when I heard you claim your father like that, something broke in me; all these years I could have been claiming my father, too, and now I feel like he just died yesterday. And it hurts so much. I miss him so much."

"I know, Tish, I know." Lavia soothed her as best as she could with her words and her tone. And then, even though neither of them was the touchy-feely type, Lavia pulled Tish to her and Tish rested her head on Lavia's shoulder and sobbed.

When Tish finished crying, they traded stories of their

growing-up years, lingering over anecdotes of messes they'd made that their parents sometimes cleaned up for them; other times, they were left to suffer the consequences, to learn from the consequences. They were especially gentle with those memories, as if they needed to return each precious one to its own space on a reachable shelf to be retrieved whenever they needed guidance. Even at this point in their lives, as sexagenarians, when they thought they should know all they needed to know, the hunger to fill in not-knowing was insatiable still.

Tish sat up excitedly and pointed at an icicle hanging from the majestic oak outside her window. "Look, there's a rainbow in that icicle; oh my god, what a beautiful thing to be trapped in ice."

"It's hardly trapped," Lavia said. "Just a band of light showing off how splendid it can be when it allows itself to bend."

Sixteen

Cynthia listened to workers spreading ice melt along her front walkway and wondered if it was safe to go outside. They'd pretreated the day before and now the freezing rain had subsided though the ice still gleamed like diamonds on the trees and the grass. She'd told Tish she would come over today. Finally. Cynthia had declined Tish's several invitations until now. They'd not really spoken since the change in relationships: Bloc and Cynthia's, Bloc and Tish's. Cynthia had been spending more time at E and Melanie's condo in town helping them get the baby's room set up and in the process learning how baby care had evolved: no crib bumpers; no blankets in the crib; they no longer sleep on their stomachs; no, they don't drink water. Plus she and Melanie's mother were planning the baby shower that they'd moved up to next week at Melanie's insistence because she said she wasn't sure but her Braxton Hicks contractions were feeling like the real thing even though she still had almost six weeks to go.

She returned from E and Melanie's last night because of the storm forecast. This morning she had a message from Tish saying she'd completely understand if she needed to take a pass today because of the weather. Cynthia told her it would be a game-time decision. She really wanted to go, wanted to get the awkwardness over with. Plus she knew Bloc wouldn't be there, he'd stayed in Philly last night with his daughter and grand-children. It was better for Bloc not to be there the first time Cynthia and Tish were spending time together since everything that happened.

Cynthia could hear icicles falling onto the patio off the bedroom, a positive sign that it was getting warmer. She tex-ted Tish that she was going to give it try, asked her what time was good. Tish replied, *Nobody here but us chickens. But let them resalt my walkway. I'll hit you up when it looks walkable.* Cynthia knew the chickens were Tish and Lavia. Lavia and Cynthia had had lunch several times, met for coffee just as of-ten. The other day they'd nestled into a secluded booth at the Throw Back where Lavia captivated Cynthia with her stories of growing up on a cruise ship, playing dress-up and pretend-ing to be royalty, protecting her parents always because they feared being carted away by the government even as they grew old. They also talked about Tish. Lavia detailed how Tish's moods had been all over the place, throwing expansive parties, then cloistering herself. But Lavia assured Cynthia that it likely had more to do with something Tish was grappling with than anything having to do with Bloc. "I mean let's face it, Tish is Tish, she's not the type to get devastated over a man, nothing against Bloc, you know I love Bloc, but they weren't in it for the long haul."

Cynthia was relieved to hear that, then asked Lavia what else was going on with Tish. "You know how years ago, when the power went out, and then came back on suddenly," Lavia said, "the surge of electricity could damage your electronics. I think she's having a surge of something from her past, and her hard drive is a little wacky. But you know, she'll unplug it and reboot and I think she'll be okay."

"You're telling my story," Cynthia said, as she went on to talk about her devastating senior year at Penn. And how she hadn't thought about it much, but since she'd moved here she was having those surges of recollections from that time. It sometimes threw her off-kilter.

"What happened?" Lavia asked. Cynthia danced around the specifics, said that she had a relationship that didn't end well.

"Not the guy who took the rap for your shoplifting attempt?"

"Oh, no, no, no, no. Not him. This man was older."

"A student?"

"No, he'd come to give a talk. October 24th, 1975, the worst night of my life. You know, he smiled at me, and I melted, and I've been blaming myself for the consequences for decades. But shit, I was like nineteen, you know. I'm realizing he was as responsible as me, if not more so."

"Shit, you were nineteen, I'm going with more so," Lavia said.

Cynthia nodded and also clamped her lips shut so that she wouldn't say more.

She thought about that conversation now as she looked at a sketch of her mother hanging on her bedroom wall. She tried to shrug off the regret of telling Lavia as much as she had, though it wasn't really much. "Was it, Mommy?" she asked the sketch the way she sometimes talked to Divine.

. . .

The sketch had been drawn the day that Gabriella met Divine for the first time. Cynthia and Gabriella rushed from school to get to Cynthia's grandmother's house to see the *Edge of Night* because Friday's episode had been a cliff-hanger. The television wasn't on and Rose was not sitting in her regular chair with a perfect view to her stories but was instead squeezed into the corner of the couch, her head resting on the couch arm.

They dropped their books and ran to her, and she lifted her head slowly and said that she was feeling a little under the weather, maybe it was the sudden heat this late in October. Then she looked at the Mickey Mouse clock atop the case still crowded with Cynthia's favorite childhood books and said, "Lord have mercy, I done missed the beginning of my story, get the TV on."

They were relieved then as they fussed over her, brought her water, dragged the coffee table to her, and put a pillow on it and propped her feet. Then Gabriella pulled Cynthia into the kitchen and whispered, "Gramum needs a doctor 'cause her feet are swollen, which could mean fluid retention, which could also mean congestive heart failure 'cause she's also perspiring a lot." Gabriella said she knew this because a similar thing had happened to her mother's aunt and her mother still faulted herself for ignoring it.

Cynthia's own heart started palpitating at the thought. "We need to call her doctor; we need to get my mom," she said, grabbing the wall phone in the kitchen and dialing and pressing the phone back in the receiver trying hard to restrain herself so as not to slam it. "It's busy, she takes it off the hook when she doesn't want to be bothered."

"Well, I'll go get her, you call the doctor, but if Gramum seems like she's getting worse, dial zero. What's your address again?"

Cynthia told her the address. "It'll be the darkest house on the block 'cause she's likely got the blinds closed tight," she said, surprising herself that she'd said that much about Divine.

"So the dark ain't never scared me," Gabriella replied, as she walked back through the living room and stopped to smooch Rose's forehead and then was out the door.

The blinds at Divine's house were closed. No one answered the bell. Gabriella knocked, still no answer. She looked around the porch absent cushioned gliders and rocking chairs. Just a metal bench centering a small clay pot where a geranium showed off a bright red bloom next to a dish holding a single cigarette butt. She lifted the pot, the dish, looking for a spare key. Then prayed there would be one under the mat. The key was there. She engaged the key, then hesitated before turning it, trying to prepare herself.

She took a deep breath and turned the key and pushed open the door and stepped into the vestibule that was black and white tiled. She opened the vestibule door into the living room. All seemed in order even in the absence of light, no bras or stockings or men's boxers hastily tossed. She chided herself for having had that image, telling herself that she was as bad as the girls who taunted Cynthia about her mother. "Miss Divine," she called. She stopped. She could hear knocking sounds coming from upstairs as if someone was repeatedly banging against a wall. She wondered if Divine was up there with a man right now. Was this how sex sounded? Gabriella didn't know how sex sounded. She was a virgin still, joking to Cynthia once that she was delaying going all the way for as long as possible, maybe until twenty-one, because she was like a black widow spider and whichever boy she'd do it with would in short order meet his maker. Not at her own hands, though; she feared her uncles would find out and kill the poor boy.

She walked to the foot of the stairs. Pushed her voice out and up and shouted this time, "Miss Divine, it's about your mother."

The knocking stopped. She could hear the release of mattress springs, feet against the floor pattering toward the top of the stairs. "What?" she called. "Who is it? What about my mother?"

"I'm Cynthia's friend Gabriella and Cynthia is with her now, but your mom's feet are really swollen, and she's not feeling well and we think she needs the doctor."

"Feet are swollen? Doctor?" Divine asked in a shrill voice, all the way down the stairs now. She was in a satiny robe, white with big red hyacinth blooms. One hand held the robe together, the other hand filled with something that looked like gravel to Gabriella, bits of it glistening in her hair, her hair silky and frazzled, and in a scary display, a pasty form of it made a ring around her mouth and formed a type of plaster spit-filled beard that had begun to harden. She dropped the gravel bits into her robe pocket, then tied her robe and rubbed her hands together, and the dust from her hands made Gabriella cough as she wondered what she'd just interrupted Divine from doing, certainly not sex, unless she'd just been screwing the sandman.

As if she read Gabriella's mind, Divine said, "I eat a little starch every now and then, so what." She wiped at her mouth and grabbed the phone from the stand next to the plastic-covered couch. "Shit, it's off the hook upstairs," she said, as she ran back up the stairs.

Gabriella wasn't easily shocked, having grown up with her uncles' stories that were bizarre and outrageous, scary, sad, and hilarious. But right now she was shocked. Starch? She'd heard about people eating starch. That was not starch. Her feet felt cemented to the carpeted floor and she just stood there trying to figure it out as she listened to Divine upstairs shouting into the phone, "Her chest? They're there now, oxygen? All right, Cynthia, just be calm and get in the ambulance with her and hold her hand. Mommy's coming. University Hospital right? I'm on the way." Divine then called Yellow Cab and groaned, "Twenty minutes, thought y'all was supposed to be so fast. Yes, yes I want the cab, what do you think I'm calling you for."

Gabriella heard water running, then heard Divine's footsteps and loud mutterings of "Father have mercy, please Jesus, please." And then just like that she was back downstairs, transformed, hair pulled up in a French twist, face cleaned, red lipstick on, pink-and-white seersucker belted shirtwaist dress, black patent high-heeled shoes to match the oversized black patent purse that she grabbed from the dining room table. "My keys, do I have my keys?" she said more to herself than to Gabriella as she pulled at the clasp but her hands were shaking and she thrust the purse at Gabriella. "Can you, please? My hands are sweating, Jesus."

Gabriella quickly opened the purse, glad to be asked to do something because she otherwise didn't know what to do. The purse smelled of Wrigley's spearmint gum and Kool cigarettes, and she could see the green of both as Divine asked her if her keys were in there and Gabriella pulled up the key ring and showed it to her.

"Okay, let's wait for the cab on the porch. You coming?" she said, walking with astonishing speed in those heels as Gabriella followed quickly behind her.

The porch was a relief. The day pulsed against them the way it had not in Divine's light-starved living room. Out here Gabriella could see that Divine and Cynthia had identical noses that were sharp, and lips that were full. But Divine's eyes were lighter than Cynthia's, her complexion, too; her hair was straighter and her hips were slim.

"So you're Gabriella, I heard about you," Divine said, as she pulled the gum from her purse and nudged it toward Gabriella.

Gabriella shook her head, declining, then said, "But if you offer me a one of those Kool filter tips, I will accept that."

"Well, good, 'cause I'm not offering." Divine made a *tsk*ing sound as she pulled the cigarette pack from her purse and shook one out. "Are you asking?"

"Yes, uh, please." Gabriella nodded, and Divine handed the pack to Gabriella. "Don't go telling your people I let you smoke," she said, as she clicked her lighter and offered the flame to Gabriella. "I know your uncle Nathan and he don't play when it comes to you."

"He really liked you," Gabriella said, as she pulled the smoke deep into her lungs.

"I liked him, too." Gabriella thought she saw a hint of blush soften the dramatic curve of Divine's cheekbones when she said that. "But I also got to keep it real. You're pretty," Divine said then. "Are you as smart as my Cynthia?"

"Nobody's as smart as Cynthia," Gabriella said, as she watched Divine turn into a peacock and toss her head and throw her shoulders back and beam.

"She gets it from her daddy," she said as she flicked her ash in the dish on the bench. "She ever tell you about him?"

"No, she never has."

"Humph."

"I mean he never came up," Gabriella rushed to offer. "I guess I never talk about my father much, either, probably 'cause he's in Mississippi."

"Doing what?"

"Living his life. My mom said he was too country for Philly and she was too Philly for the backwoods, and they couldn't settle on a place in the middle so he's there and she's here, but I spend part of the summer with him every year."

"That's good you spend time with him. I wish Cynthia would. Her daddy's constantly begging for her to come to where he is."

"Where is he?"

"Japan. Air Force. I'm surprised Cynthia never mentioned him. He writes her five-, six-page letters once a month like clockwork. He shot up through the ranks like a meteor he's such a smart man, a real wiz. I told Cynthia she should go. She's tethered to her grandmother, though." She stopped herself. She closed her eyes and said, "Lord, please let her be okay, if not for me, for Cynthia."

"Well, for you, too," Gabriella countered.

Divine hunched her shoulders and looked toward the street. "Where the hell is the cab?" she muttered, as she mashed her cigarette in the dish and sat on the bench between the smoldering ash and the blood-red geranium.

"Cynthia may not talk about her dad," Gabriella said, leaping back in the conversation. "But she talks about you all the time." She didn't know why she'd just made that up like that. "All the time, she's always going on and on about how tight y'all are."

"You telling a lie—"

"I swear to God and three other white men, as Uncle Nathan would say."

Divine stared ahead. Her face was fixed as if she wanted to break out in a smile but refused. Gabriella thought that when she sat down to sketch Divine, this is the expression she'd capture: her mouth with the pouty lips, not curved, but not clamped, either; her cheeks not expanded into blooms, but at least her jaw was no longer clenched; and her eyes that were set back as if they'd been fashioned by a dollmaker at Mattel no longer had that anxious pointedness, instead settled into a remarkable softness. Though Gabriella mostly worked in pencil, charcoal, or ink, she thought this once she'd dip her finger in a little red paint to render the geranium, still fierce this late in the season. Thought, too, that she'd hang just a hint of color along Divine's cheekbones to highlight the absence of the smile wanting to be.

. . .

Gabriella had finally given the portrait to Cynthia only three years ago, before she left for Santa Fe. She'd had it framed in non-reflective glass. Cynthia cried for weeks every time she looked at it gracing the center of the mantel. She felt like crying now as she looked at it hanging on a wall of its own in her bedroom where she could see it first thing when she woke and last thing before she went to sleep. She thought Gabriella a genius in the way she'd captured Divine right before she'd unleash her smile. But not that smile that Cynthia dreaded that Divine would flash when she was so up, so unmoored, and blazed with so much fire that Cynthia imagined her smile alone could usher in the Rapture and raise the dead. She certainly raised the nature of whichever man she chose to snag with that smile. Any man would do when she was manic like that. It didn't matter whether he taught at Cynthia's school, or went to Rose's church, or had spent the day working on the roof of the house next door, or cut hair on Sixtieth Street, or was the father of one, two, three of her classmates—they could have all been the same man because they blurred over time.

It was the promise of that other smile that Gabriella had

captured. The one Cynthia lived for. Maybe it was when Divine hummed as she cooked dinner. Perhaps it was a spaghetti night and Cynthia might look up from her black-and-white composition book as she enjoyed the smell of mushrooms and green peppers and onions coming together in the pan. Divine might turn from the stove in that same instant and rest her long-handled wooden spoon on the plate and look at Cynthia and smile with her entire face so that even her saucer eyes got in on the smile and relaxed; her dramatic cheekbones blossomed; her full mouth curved perfectly like an upside-down rainbow pointing to the pot of gold. It was a smile that said I love you from a place that is so deep that it is still forming; it is light-years from even having a name. That was the smile.

Cynthia's phone buzzed then. It was Gabriella.

"Girl, you gonna live a long time," Cynthia said as she pushed her pods into her ears. "I was just thinking about you. I was looking at the sketch you did of Mommy and am reminded again of your genius."

"That's why I'm calling," Gabriella said, as Cynthia nestled on her chaise, enjoying the sound of Gabriella's voice.

"You calling 'bout the sketch? I know you not asking for it back," Cynthia laughed.

"I'm calling 'bout my genius."

"Go on and brag, I'm here for it," Cynthia said.

"First, tell me what you were getting ready to do."

"I was getting ready to go to Tish's, why?"

"Remember what my Uncle Hal used to say about how when

something happens that upends you, consider the thing you were about to do before it happened, then as much as you can, do that?" Gabriella said.

Cynthia sat up slowly. "Gab, what's happened? Are the triplets okay? My goddaughter? You? What? What is it?"

"It's nothing like that, everybody's well. It's just that I got to tell you something."

"Okay," Cynthia felt dizzy.

"You know I hate going back to that night," Gabriella said.

"Well, then don't," Cynthia interrupted, knowing what that night meant—the night with Mr. Z.

"I wouldn't otherwise, but, it could come up, and I want you to be prepared, 'cause forewarned is forearmed."

"What are you saying, Gab?"

"Remember the pictures of his family in his wallet? I'm pretty sure that was her—"

"Who, her?"

"Tish, I'm pretty sure that's her in the picture—"

"Wait, what?"

"His daughter."

"Daughter? Gab, hell no."

"I pretty much knew from that first selfie you texted when you first moved there with the four of you—"

"Stop it, Gab, fucking stop it—"

"And I sketched out how she may have looked, you know in the 1970s—"

"Wait, wait, wait, Tish's last name is Jones. Mr. Z's last name is Willis. I can't believe I just said his name out loud. You're wrong—"

"Well does she talk about her father?"

"No, so, what the hell?"

"So, I'm pretty sure that's her, that's so-what-the-hell."

"How sure is pretty sure?" Cynthia could hardly breathe.

"Sure enough that I'm even telling you. Would I drop some shit like this this on you otherwise, Cynt?"

Cynthia's phone pinged then with a text from Tish saying that her walkway had been cleared, and that Cynthia should come now before it froze again. "Shit, that's her texting now. How am I even supposed to go—how am I supposed to act?"

"Listen to me, Cynt, you go." Gabriella said. "You act normal. I mean whatever normal is between y'all, given what happened with you and Bloc. . . . Just do that, Cynt. Do that. You go on over to Tish's, and you just let things be."

Gabriella talked in a soothing tone. Cynthia allowed Gabriella's voice to calm her the way it always could, the way it had that night.

By the time their call ended, Cynthia's phone was in the red; she started to charge it but then decided to plug it in at Tish's. The sun was close to falling and she didn't want the paths to refreeze. She put on extra socks and then pulled on the ski pants Melanie had bought for her as part of a Christmas gift that was to include a ski trip, even though Cynthia didn't ski, but that was the year she fell down her steps anyhow so the trip was put on hold. She stuffed her feet into her snow boots, her arms into her ski jacket, then pulled on her gloves and hat, slipped her phone in her pocket, and was out the door.

The walk from Cynthia's cottage to Tish's usually took

Cynthia five minutes that could stretch to ten if she stopped to chat with neighbors she encountered or took her time to admire the vegetation along the way that changed gloriously with the seasons. Today she slowed her pace to attempt to absorb what Gabriella had just said, that Tish was Mr. Z's daughter. It was eerily quiet, as if the ice were securing secrets that would otherwise float through the air revealing themselves. She surrendered to the quiet; surrendered to the truth that she now knew what had caused her dizzy spell as Lavia and Tish argued about Tish's father and prostitutes.

It was so quiet that Cynthia thought she could hear the twirling sounds the jewels of ice made as they clung to the tree branches like the crystal drops on a grand chandelier. She could almost smell the ammonia she and her mother had used that day to clean her grandmother's chandelier in the immediate aftermath of Cynthia's time with Mr. Z. It was if her mother had clawed through her own mental health issues and acquired miraculous discernment to know that Cynthia needed to keep her hands busy so that her mind could be still.

The chandelier took the entire Saturday. They first had to remove the bulbs and cover the sockets with masking tape so cleaning fluid wouldn't spill in. Then they detached all the crystal drops suspended by minuscule hooks that had to be separated from the crystal drops. They soaked the drops in ammonia solution and dusted the hooks, and Cynthia used a ladder to tackle the chandelier, cleaning it in its intricate places that were beautiful, but that also held the dust that had accumulated over the years into a tufted grime. "From top to bottom, inside out," her mother coached. "Yeah, beautiful, you're doing a beautiful job, Cynthia." They rinsed and shined the delicate crystal drops together, then reinserted each onto its tiny hook. Cynthia took to the ladder again and attached the now-gleaming crystal parts, one at a time, carefully because they were delicate, as her mother whispered, "Good, top to bottom, inside to out."

After Cynthia had screwed in the light bulbs, Divine called for a drumroll as her grandmother flicked the wall switch and the room was suddenly cast in a more dazzling light. A more purified light that seemed to illuminate an elegant innocence everywhere it fell.

By now, Cynthia had reached the pond that was nearly adjacent to Tish's cottage. The pond was shocked to stillness, covered as it was in a thick, smooth glaze of shame that it had allowed itself to be overtaken by the freezing rain, by the cold. Cynthia moved off the cleared path and inched toward the pond. She held on to the sturdy base of the pussy willow tree to ease herself down to sit. She pulled her hood over her head. She hugged her knees toward her and buried her head in her circled arms that seemed to be waiting for her to do that. The fox fur rimming her jacket hood stroked her cheeks as if saying, *Come on, come on, top to bottom, inside to out. Come on.* She did, finally. She allowed herself to see the whole of it from the inside.

Seventeen

I f only she hadn't gone to Mr. Z's lecture and returned his smile when he took to the stage. If only Macon hadn't asked for an understanding, if only her mother had been normal then she would have never sat on Macon's steps that day and fallen in love with him.

She was exhausted that day. The day before, she'd received her monthly I-love-you-daughter letter from her father, who was stationed in Japan. This time in addition to the check he always sent Divine, he asked for more than a visit from Cynthia, he asked if they'd consider moving there. Cynthia could finish high school there, which would have the added benefit of making her even more attractive to the elite universities.

Divine read the letter out loud, perched on Cynthia's bed as Cynthia set her mother's hair with bright pink sponge rollers. Cynthia was ecstatic at the prospect. She had the vaguest memories of her father living with them. Remembered most the swirl of the air when she'd jump into his arms and he'd spin her around and around. She'd throw her arms out with abandon, laughing wildly, knowing that his hold would keep her safe.

She hardly breathed she listened so intently as Divine read. She thought she could even hear the smile in Divine's voice when she read the part about how to this day, there was no equal to her, no one had come close to capturing his heart the way she had.

"That's sweet, he's sweet," Divine said when she'd finished reading. "But of course it won't work."

"But it can, though," Cynthia said. "We could even convince Gramum to come."

"I'm no good for him. And he's too good."

"But you're good, too, Mommy, you could be good together." Cynthia fought to keep the desperation from her voice as Divine pulled her head away from Cynthia's hands. "I'm not finished rolling your hair," Cynthia said. "Come on, Mommy, let me finish your hair, and we can at least talk about it."

"It's okay," Divine said, moving off the bed to the yelping sounds the bedsprings made, as if they were crying on Cynthia's behalf. Crying on Divine's behalf, too, as she stood and Cynthia could see that her mother's perfectly shaped oval face was suddenly puffed up, as if all her feelings were trapped right there in her cheeks and under her eyes and around her mouth.

"No, it's not okay. Come on, Mommy. Sit back down and let me finish your hair, please," Cynthia begged. "And anyhow, think about how good you've been here lately, think about all of this." Cynthia pointed to the flouncy curtains hanging at her window. She and Divine had picked out the fabric together, measured and cut the material to size, stitched the edges, pleated the hem, even found curtain rods in that aqua shade to hang them on. The afterglow of the project had so far lasted for a several-month-long stretch when there was no listening to Divine banging on the wall half the night as she tore out its substance like a madwoman; no shut blinds putting the living room into a perpetual state of night. No Divine gushing that inappropriate smile when she came onto a man.

The past few months had been so answered-prayer normal that Cynthia had even had no need to ask her mother to sleep in her room. She'd almost joined in with the snooty girls' recitations of their moms' this and that to say, *Me and Mom made curtains to match my blue-green bedspread and my paisley bureau lampshade, and my hook-stitch step-on rug. My mom said my bedroom is so put-together it should be on the cover of* Seventeen. She held back, though; deep down she knew that the normal would not last.

So Cynthia sat on Macon's steps and allowed his breath transformed through metal to pounce against her until it penetrated her skin and melted to a warm liquid inside her. His music was all she had in that moment. Gabriella and Cassie were visiting Gabriella's father; her grandmother was on a church excursion to the Gullah Festival. So when the music stopped, it was so easy to follow him into his house and up the stairs to his bedroom.

"I been looking at you for years," he said as he extended his hand toward a cracked vinyl ottoman next to his bed.

"I've been listening to you for years," she replied, as he sat on his bed and she watched him roll a joint with astounding deftness given the limited use of his arm paralyzed by polio. He offered the joint to her, and she shook her head no, and he said, "Well, in that case, I'll hold up, too, Cynthia? Right?" He raised his eyebrows and something about the look of them was so pure that she wanted to cry.

"I know that's your name 'cause I hear your grandmom talking about you to Miss Millie next door. 'My Cynthia is in the exceptional class, my Cynthia got straight A's, my Cynthia could get into Harvard if she wants. My Cynthia is such a good girl.'"

"She likes to brag. I think she does it to compensate for my mom." Cynthia couldn't believe she'd just said that. She otherwise never talked about her mother. "And your name is Macon, right?" She rushed the question to move on from her mother.

"It is. And I bet you don't hear too many neighbors bragging on me. Your grandmom claiming Harvard for you. They just cracked the door enough for me to slip into Temple."

"You going to Temple?"

"Leaving next week for orientation. Music scholarship covers room and board so I'm jumping on all of that."

"Uh, congratulations. I'll miss hearing you play," she said.

"And I'll miss your ear."

"My ear? How about my eyes, or my smile, but my ear?" She was proud of herself that she'd come up with that line.

"I'd like to miss your smile, but I've never seen it."

She looked down then. She wished she was one of those self-assured girls who could keep a repartee going and flirt and lead boys on. But those girls were mostly pretty. "My smile's nothing special."

"I beg to differ, my bent arm is nothing special." He reached out and took her chin in his hand and lifted her face.

She marveled at his ability to be so open about the parts of himself that would make people look away, his bent arm, his foot that turned inward. She wondered if he saw that ugly girl part of her and was captivated nonetheless. She tilted her face like an invitation and he leaned in and kissed her. He nudged her onto the bed and lay next to her. The rotating fan clinked like a love song as he half whispered, half sang, come on, come on, come on, until his fingers made the rivers crest and the flooding took her under.

After Gabriella told Cynthia that Macon was cute, and Cassie said that he had a kind heart, and Gabriella's Uncle Nathan pulled him aside and told him, "Hey, young blood, you seem cool so I say this with nothing but brotherly love. I am licensed to carry, so you hurt her in any way shape or form, your mother will have to have a closed casket 'cause that's how bad I'll fuck you up. With love, my brother" . . . after that, Macon became Cynthia's dream of a boyfriend, so she was devastated years later, when she was in her senior year of college and Macon, who had graduated from Temple, took her to breakfast and stammered over his eggs and toast.

"Understanding? You want us to have an understanding?" Cynthia raised her brows in a question as they ate buttered toast at the diner on Walnut Street. "What's to understand? Do you mean as in the Jerry Butler song 'Ain't Understanding Mellow'?"

"Not exactly like that, but in a way like that," he whispered. "It's like we both know we'd never intentionally hurt each other. But say I call you and I want to come over and you tell me it's not a good time; I'll draw on my understanding of the situation that maybe you met someone earlier, maybe he's in your psych class, maybe y'all walk home together and you invite him up for, I don't know, a grilled cheese sandwich."

"Definitely not grilled cheese. Who invites someone up for grilled cheese?"

"Okay, a cup of java, a glass of juice, I don't know—"

"Are you breaking up with me?" she'd asked, demanding of herself that she not cry, not become a spectacle in the restaurant.

"I'm not breaking up with you. I just don't want to put you in the position where you feel constrained, you know. I haven't been available lately, been doing a lot of gigs—"

"So that's her name, Gigs?"

"Cynthia, you not being fair—"

"Me not being fair, you saying you want to see other people and I'm the one not being fair?" Her voice shrieked. She quickly lowered it. "Consider this. You and me . . ." She separated her downward-facing palms, the international sign language symbol for *all done.*

Then she cried over a middle-of-the-night bowl of cereal with Gabriella, who consoled Cynthia that maybe it wasn't the worst thing; Macon was being honest at least and not trying to creep. Her roommates chimed in that Macon had a point. Nothing wrong with testing the waters, see what the waves were like on the other side of the peninsula.

Cynthia softened. She called Macon between her classes the next day and said they could try his understanding thing. She didn't see a good outcome, but they could try.

She vacillated the rest of the day from feeling angry, to rejected, to sad, to slightly hopeful. She was back to angry as Macon slid in next to her just as Mr. Z took the stage. She felt Gabriella's elbow in her side telling her to be kind. Gabriella had managed to save the

209

entire row for Mr. Z's lecture because Cynthia said her roommates and friends from her poly sci class were also coming, friends from her urban studies class; friends. Her mother's issues had not been a barrier here to her forming friendships. There were so many other barriers that sprang up for the Black students here that connected them automatically, fused them. They'd nod at one another in an otherwise all-white lecture hall, acknowledging with the slight bow of the head, *you are not alone; I'm here too, here for you.* They all sat together in the dining hall turning a deaf ear to accusations of self-segregation, preferring to label it self-preservation. Cynthia didn't feel the need to hide inside herself lest she be whispered about. She didn't have to work for approval. The acceptance was all around her like air; she just needed to take it in.

She took it in at that moment. She settled deeper into her seat as Mr. Z approached the lectern. Macon covered her hand with his and she remembered how he'd covered her hand when they'd gone to the movies the first time. They'd seen *Love Story* and he'd leaned in and whispered in her ear that he loved her. That day she could feel the indentations in his fingertips caused by his constant flute-playing. But sitting there next to her at the lecture his fingers were smooth as lard. She eased her hand from under his and folded her hands in her own lap like the good girl that she was, that her grandmother told her she was, her teachers, and Miss Cassie and the uncles, and Reverend Grant, who'd baptized her when she was twelve and prayed over her before she moved to the dorm; such a good girl. She caressed her own hands, surprised at how warm they were. Thought that they should be cold as winter since Macon's smooth-as-lard fingers told her what she already knew, that he hadn't had gigs lately. Her hands should be colder still sensing as she was that Mr. Z's eyes were fixed on her. They were. His mouth shaped in a smile like bacon curving in a cast-iron pan, plump, sizzling.

Cynthia returned his smile, telling herself that she was just being polite, he was a Black man, after all, giving a talk at this elite university. How much shit had he had to plow through in his day to get here? Mr. Z more than earned her polite, good-girl smile. Except that the smile she flashed was neither polite nor good-girlish. She tilted her head the way she'd watch Divine's head tilt when she had designs on a man: she lowered her eyes and raised one brow; she allowed just the corners of her mouth to lift so that her lips remained pursed, her cheeks blossomed. When she'd watch her mother put on that look for a man, Cynthia thought it not a smile, but an offering. She told herself this was different. He was up there on the stage; she was sitting here with her maybe-boyfriend. She was safe.

Mr. Z opened by intoning that despite his reputation, he was not at war with white people, though he was at war with the systems that deny Black people a slice of the economic pie. "Let me be for real, here," he said, his eyes scanning the auditorium. "In a perfect society, I would much rather make love than war." Applause then, hoots, shouts of yes, yes. His eyes fell on Cynthia and held there. He repeated it then. "Let's make love not war."

His eyes moved on. Cynthia's reaction to the feel of them did not. She felt new as she watched him move away from the lectern and pace the stage, pausing to fling back his camel-colored jacket showing off his oversized peace sign belt buckle. She forced herself to look away from him, wondering if this is how her mother felt when she yearned after a man. *Yearning, is that what this is?* she asked herself. She yearned for leather boots she couldn't afford, the butter brickle ice cream cone that would blow up her calorie count; she yearned for self-assurance, a normal mother, a father who lived in the same city as she. She knew yearning. Yearning didn't step up her heart rate like this, or make her suddenly aware of her bra pushing against her breasts . . . or was it the other way around? Yearning didn't unleash a trickle that grew into a pulsing that caused her to shift in her seat right now and cross and uncross her legs so much that Macon asked her if she was okay. She nodded and touched his arm. She was suddenly grateful that he'd asked for an understanding. No need to be guilt-ridden about this newness she was experiencing that she'd politely named yearning. This wasn't yearning. This was deeper, as if something at her core had been aroused, spinning now, pulling her into its churn.

She tried to concentrate on what Mr. Z was saying as he moved to the guts of his presentation. What was he saying? Something about the demise of Black neighborhoods being an intentional strategy to keep Black people from transferring wealth to the next generation. The tragedy of Black people leaving property to their heirs that was worth less than what they paid because of government-sanctioned redlining, and other forms of housing discrimination. "Black people transfer to the next generation not wealth, but deficits," he boomed. Gabriella went to church then and clapped and called out, "You telling the truth." Cynthia settled herself, relieved that she was hearing the gist of it. They would talk about it later as they all gathered at her campus apartment. They would pass joints and drink cheap fruity wine and listen to War and Stevie Wonder and reconcile the munchies with Italian hoagies from Ronnie's Steak Shop.

Mr. Z concluded his talk to a rousing ovation and Gabriella rushed to shake his hand and tell him how much her uncle Nathan loved his work, and how she could identify as she described for him where she lived in West Philly, and how her family had been the first Black people to move onto their block and then all the white people moved out as if they would catch smallpox if they did not. Cynthia had inched up to stand right next to Gabriella. She was looking at the cleft in Mr. Z's chin, the black turtleneck he wore under the camel-colored jacket, the wide-wale corduroy pants. Then she tried to contain a gasp as she listened to Gabriella invite him over. "My friend Cynthia lives on campus, and we're all assembling there in just a bit. We'd love for you to join us, wouldn't we, Cynthia?"

"Well, would we, Cynthia?" he asked, as he focused on Cynthia and she picked up his eyes that were a light shade of brown. Or were they really darker, but appeared lighter because of the spark that suddenly shone when he looked at her. "Yes, yes, of course, we'd be honored if you dropped by."

"Well, I think the university has prepared a bit of a reception but I'd be delighted to stop by after."

"I'll see that he gets there," Macon said, who'd joined the circle. And Gabriella grabbed Cynthia's arm and said, "Okay, we're gonna tidy the apartment since we're having such a special guest."

When they'd gotten out of earshot of the burgeoning group of people waiting to greet Mr. Z, Gabriella said, "Girl, I thought I was gonna have to grab a fire extinguisher to quell the heat shooting out of that man when he looked at you."

Cynthia rolled her eyes in her head and Gabriella said, "You do know I'm a student of faces, right? And I'm not just talking about my memory for a face that I may have seen once ten years ago, I'm talking about interpreting what a face says. And the man's face was saying some x-rated shit."

"Well, why did you invite him over then, he's old enough to be my father."

"Trust me, he is, from his bio, which ends with mention of a wife and kid might I add, he's close to fifty if not older. I invited him for the conversation only. Plus I know Macon will have his face in the place; you did notice how quick he was to say, 'I'll see that he gets there.'" She imitated Macon and they laughed. Gabriella added that Macon made sure to take the seat next to Cynthia. "Macon's only got eyes for you, Cynt. His asking for an understanding doesn't change that."

When they returned to Cynthia's apartment in the high-rise dorm, one of her roommates was already there pouring chips into a bowl as that one's boyfriend rolled stogies. Gabriella announced that Mr. Z was stopping by and the boyfriend looked up over the tops of his glasses. "Is he gonna be cool with all this?"

"Maybe we should move this party to the lounge," Cynthia

said, and they all agreed as they gathered cups and wine and napkins and headed for the lounge.

. . .

News of the gathering spread. The lounge quickly filled with people bringing more wine, Pagano's Pizza, Gino's fried chicken with biscuits; bringing laughter, bringing music by Sly and Marvin Gaye, Stevie Wonder, James Brown, Patti LaBelle; bringing their unmasked unburdened selves, their not-giving-a-fuck-right-now selves because they'd made it through yet another day of riding the rough white waves without going under. Plus, they'd just listened to a phenomenal Black man give a talk that represented some of their own thoughts. And soon, as the music blared and the dancing started, and the wine was swallowed, the joints smoked, the food devoured, the fifty or so people crammed in the lounge didn't even care that the VIP guest had not yet shown. Their interconnectedness was more than enough.

Macon finally arrived; Mr. Z was not with him. Cynthia was both disappointed and relieved. His presence would have been a thrill, but also a complication. She was back to hopeful about her relationship with Macon as she watched him push into the room with the beautiful asymmetry of his gait, watched his eyes scan the lounge until he found Cynthia, saw the look of delight that always hung in his eyes when he'd see her. She got a surge then, tried to convince herself that it far exceeded the surge of desire Mr. Z's attention had sparked.

"I gave your boy the address to your dorm apartment since

I thought that's where things were going down. He'll see the lounge first though. Might show, might not," Macon whispered in Cynthia's ear.

His breath was a warm comfort and she leaned in closer. "When he'd get to be my boy?" she asked.

"I saw how he looked at you, made a comment about you after you walked away and I was almost ready to put my foot up his old ass."

Cynthia laughed and stroked his arm. "I'm glad you did not assault the man. And I'm glad you came back even if he didn't. You wanna spend the night?"

"Actually, I gotta slide from here right now. Gotta gig that's gonna run way past midnight. Hope to be done before the sun is up. Anyhow I thought Gab was staying."

"She is. But both the roomies are crashing at their boyfriends' so, you know, if you want to, no pressure."

"I like pressure, baby doll, I'll see if I can show through but it's gonna be late, or should I say early, 'cause it might be dawn," he said as he winked. She watched him edge through the crowded lounge and dance a couple of steps to the door. She marveled again at the deftness of his moves even with his foot that dragged, the bend in his arm.

After the party thinned, Gabriella helped Cynthia pick up trash and otherwise restore the lounge to its original tweediness. She asked Cynthia if it was okay if she grabbed a pillow and blanket and slept in the lounge because she needed the buzz of a television turned on low to sleep well. Cynthia told her to have at it, and to just be sure that she put a sheet over the couch before she lay down because who knew what horrors lurked there, adding that anyway, there would be a rubber band on her doorknob. Gabriella's eyes got big. She already knew that Cynthia and her roommates used the rubber band on the doorknob to signal, *I got company, do not enter my bedroom.* "Aha," she said, "I knew Macon had a self-assured grin leaving here tonight. Glad my ass will be out here on this couch so I don't need no earplugs. But I do need my middle-of-the-night bowl of cereal should I wake." Cynthia left her the key to the apartment door, told her to help herself to anything in the fridge and cabinets.

After Gabriella settled in on the lounge couch, Cynthia went back down the hall to the apartment and changed from her jeans and blouse, put on her lacy-bikini panties, and a long thin semi-sheer tee. She slicked her skin with cocoa butter and spread gloss on her lips and pulled her thick hair back into an Afro puff. She felt silky inside as she affixed the rubber band on the knob to her bedroom door and turned off the light then stretched out on her bed to take a nap. She figured Macon was hours away due to what he called the set after the gig when the musicians would unwind and smoke a joint or two and riff on how the set had gone as they critiqued themselves. She wondered if that's what was really happening, wondered if actually he'd fallen in love, wondered who she was, how she looked, was she all the things Cynthia was not: tall and thin and flirty and fine. She stopped her thoughts. Got up and turned on the low desk lamp to scatter the dark air in there. She thought about just staying up and reading, then her ears perked at the chime coming from down the hall; the elevator had stopped on her floor. She tried not to hope for it to be Macon, didn't want to be disappointed even as she sensed the press of footsteps moving toward her apartment followed by a hesitation in the air right outside the door and then the tap against it. She chided herself for how distorted her thinking had just been. Macon must have headed over as soon as the set was done, maybe he'd blown it off altogether so anxious to get back to her. There was another tap and she smiled at Macon's politeness. He never assumed that he was welcome to enter the way the men seeing her roommates often did, who'd just turn the handle and knock only if the door was locked. She opened her bedroom door and ran through the slice of a living room to the front door. "I knew you'd surprise me," she called through the door. "Imma unlock the door, then you count to three and come on in to my bedroom."

She hurried back to her room and onto her bed and positioned herself as if she were a centerfold in *Jet* magazine, one leg stretched long, the other folded over showing her substantial thighs. She closed her eyes. She giggled excitedly as she heard the click of the metal tongue of the front door release from the groove. She felt a new level of eroticism in her see-through t-shirt and bikini panties, her skin slicked with cocoa butter, her lips slathered with Vaseline. She arched her back and tossed her head and pursed her mouth. She closed her eyes because she feared she might go shy and collapse inside of herself if she witnessed Macon's first reaction to the sight of her. She felt giddy with her eyes closed as she listened to the press of footsteps crossing the threshold into her bedroom. And then silence. A gasp, then followed by a voice that wasn't Macon's voice. "Jesus," the not-Macon said. She opened her eyes, and there was Mr. Z. She was too paralyzed to move.

She took in his leather loafers, the peep of argyle socks, the wide pinwale of corduroy pants, the camel-hair blazer, the plaid scarf around his neck, unloosening, hanging, the tan leather brief-case falling to the floor. She took in his wanting, felt his wanting all the way to his toes, or was it her own wanting?

His face disassembled into a mess of wanting so uncloaked he appeared as if he was about to cry; babbling like a holy man speaking in tongues until his words could form themselves and still all he managed to say was "Uh, damn, damn, damn, uh mercy, uh, look at you, lady, Jesus—"

When she recovered the next instant, she sat back on her knees and folded her arms over her chest, hiding herself the way a good girl would.

He stopped in his tracks when she did that. Shook his head back and forth then as if he'd been slapped. "Uh, you seem surprised to see me," he said. "I mean, was it me you were expecting? I thought this is where the party was—" He coughed as if his breath was caught in his throat.

"I was expecting you earlier," she said. "You know, we all were, for the get-together. A lot of people showed up."

"And just now?" he asked.

"Just now?"

"Were you expecting me just now? I mean, you said come on in—"

She wrapped her arms tighter around her chest. She could feel her fingers digging into her sides. "For the party," she said, as she took in his presence. His eyes were boyishly large for a man his age. His skin called to mind the milk chocolate icing that her grandmother whipped to an uninterrupted smoothness. Only his hair, the perfectly shaped Afro with gray strands mixing, confirmed the age Gabriella had calculated from his bio. "I was expecting you for the party. I was expecting someone else just now."

"Oh god, I'm sorry you know. Damn. Well, since I've obviously missed the party, I should leave," he said with his mouth. Though his standing there, his eyes not moving from her face, his loafers planted intractably in the tufted carpet said the opposite.

"Yeah, you should probably leave," she said, not moving, either, as she returned his stare, thinking that if she had on more than panties and a see-through tee, she'd walk him to the door.

Still he made no motion toward the door, just stood there, eyes planted on her face, waiting, she knew, for her to make a first move. She didn't know first moves. Didn't know how to say, *I wasn't expecting you but I'm sure as hell glad to see you*, or *Take down my number, some other night when you're back on campus, you can give me a call.*

She felt a clap of disappointment like thunder in her chest as he rewrapped his scarf around his neck and leaned to pick up his briefcase. He sighed resignedly then, allowing his words to ride atop the sigh. "I'd give anything right now to be that lucky guy you were expecting," he whispered. "And can I just say that I never knew I could exercise the level of self-control that it's taking for me to, you know, to leave, to leave you, because the expression on your face is driving me crazy. I mean it's like you're calling out to me with what your face is doing right now."

She wondered if he was seeing the look on her face that her mother flashed at men, signaling her wanting. She thought her mother infantile at such times, living as if she were the only one in the world who had desires, who had the right to have her desires satisfied as soon as they came down on her. No thought to the consequences of her indiscretions, the consequences that Cynthia had borne.

She told herself now that she wasn't her mother. She wasn't sneaking a man into the house that she shared with her daughter. He was from some other city and it was the middle of the night and there was a rubber band on her doorknob and no one else would ever have to know. He was safe in that way.

Her nakedness pulsed under the semisheer top with such force that she could feel it against her arms, inclining her to loosen her grip. It was a subtle move but had not gone unnoticed by Mr. Z as he blew out a long breath that was the opposite of his sigh. This was a breath of anticipation as she unfolded her arms in slow motion.

He started talking then in a rush of words as he described how he could barely get through his lecture because she'd affected him so. He peeled his jacket away, not taking his eyes from her, as if she might change her mind if he did. He sat on her bed and stroked her leg. "Hundreds of people there and all I saw was you. Damn, lady, you are so beautiful." He put her feet in his lap and pressed his thumbs against her arch. His thumb, the feel of the wide-wale corduroy against her heels, melted any lingering hesitation she might have had as he said, "God, the expression on your face, lady, during the lecture, now, oh my god, I can't stand it, please, please, let me stay, be with you." He gasped the words, as much as talked. And then it didn't matter because she reached over and clicked off the desk lamp. And just like that their breaths were mingling the tastes of scotch whisky and fruit-flavored Juicy Fruit gum, experience and innocence changing places so that none could say which was which. The sound of his peace sign belt buckle exploded in her ears as it hit the metal side of her bed. His mouth was everywhere then, setting her on fire. She opened herself completely as he moved inside of her, rearranging her purity that had been Macon's purity alone. Except that her purity had never been Macon's to claim, to own. She owned it. Owned it completely right now as she matched Mr. Z push for pull, driving him to the ends of the earth she could tell, as his breaths came so hard and fast that he sounded like a typhoon, which magnified the feel of the circles going round and round inside of her until she was spinning too. She cried out, "Jesus." And then he collapsed against her and they both went still.

She lay encircled by him while her own breaths recovered, while the residual moans pushed up from her throat like the last notes of a Smokey Robinson love song, while the tingles receded from the surface of her skin and then from inside of her and she felt both spent and light. She closed her eyes and drifted for a while to someplace between a hazy sleep and a pointed focus. Present in this bed with the weight of him heavy on top of her, seemingly all around her as she contemplated what she'd just done: she'd smiled at an older man who'd made her feel so beautiful that she'd unabashedly let him into the soft, turbulent swirl of her young womanhood, her unknowingness.

She was so unknowing she dozed off to sleep for real, thinking that she could do this again with him, and again. He could steal away from his family, his obligations. He could come to Philly, come to her. They could eat cheesesteaks and drink wine and he could detail his research about race and income disparities. He could complain about his wife the way the men having affairs on her grandmother's soap operas justified themselves. She would listen empathetically and unclasp his peace sign belt buckle and tell him he was here with her now. Let it all go and be with her. She'd do her own unburdening too. She'd tell him what she'd never told anyone about her mother: how when Divine was depressed she'd hole herself up in her room, not to be with some errant man, but to pound the hole she'd dug in the wall, to tear out chunks of plaster that glistened like fallen stars, to gnaw at the chunks with her beautiful teeth, softening the rocks to paste. To swallow? To spit out? Cynthia was never sure. Just knew that Divine would become like a madwoman, a monster, the way she'd go at that wall. She could tell him all about how it made her feel so angry and so fragile and then so almighty as she'd help her mother brush the plaster dust from her hair. He might even have some insight. Surely he'd have to keep her secret because to expose Cynthia would mean exposing himself.

She fell asleep tingling with the possibilities of a relationship with him. She woke up smiling, not sure for how long she'd slept, as the darkness smiled back at her. She thought she should nudge him; dawn would be here in no time, bringing Macon to her door. She decided against waking him, though; this is what an understanding was, right? Macon would knock on her door and she wouldn't answer and he would understand. She felt giggly inside as she lay there with Mr. Z and his stillness, and her assumptions.

Her assumptions! She assumed that all older men exploded

and then collapsed as he'd just done. And then a recognition seemed to rise from the bed and float to the ceiling. It appeared at first as a wavy line looking down on her with neither judgment nor approval, just recognition. Until she took a deep breath and the recognition was inside of her, no longer a flutter of a line so light and filled with air, but a ton of a solid mass that thudded in the center of her chest.

He was so still. He was too still. Like a statue still. Bronzed and heavy as Michelangelo's *David* still. Immovably still, rendering her immovable too. She was pinned under him entirely. His head was wedged in the crook of her neck. His arms circled her, locking her in place. She focused on her neck and willed herself to feel his breaths. There were no breaths. Just the memory of his gasps that had grown shorter and faster, just the memory of that extended breath that had seemed to lift and disperse as soon as it landed. She searched her memory to try to calculate when she'd felt that last breath. Before she'd fallen asleep. An hour? Two? How long could a person live without taking a next breath? She was trapped and paralyzed by the combination of the dead weight of him and her own terror.

She focused on the feel of his chest; was it already hardening? It couldn't be, she told herself as she tried to shift her shoulders, tried to writhe under him, tried to angle herself so that she could get a leg in position to push him off her. The harder she worked, the more he seemed to weigh. His head, his arms, were like clasps securing his upper body to her own. If she could just move his head, she thought, she could move him; she could roll him onto his back and give him mouth-to-mouth and bring him back to life.

Back to life! she screamed in her head. She couldn't bring him back to life if he was not first dead. Dead. Sweet Jesus, don't let him do this. She shouted in her head, *Don't let him die in my bed like this! Don't let him be dead. Bring him back, sweet Jesus, please bring him back.* Even as she asked it, she knew that if he was dead, there was no bringing him back. No such miracle for her this middle of the night. She remembered her grandmother's prayer then, who'd tell Cynthia that when the tempest is raging, better than praying for the storm to stop, is to pray for the Good Lord to just get in the boat with you. *Please, Father God,* she yelled in her head, *please help me, please be in this boat with me.*

She was sobbing now, so quietly, so forcefully that her whole body shook. And then like a miracle, she felt something. Movement in the air. She shut down her sobs, her thoughts, her breaths so that she could hear, feel what this movement was. It was not him. Was not. It was not even in this bedroom. It was outside, beyond the small slice of a hallway that blended into the living room where the kitchenette occupied a corner. The cabinet with the ungreased bracket that squealed like a mouse when it was swung open. The crunch of wax paper, the tings of cereal hitting a glass bowl, like a song, a victorious song; it was Gabriella getting her middle of the night snack.

"Gab, Gab," Cynthia called out in a loud whisper, trying to push her voice over the suction of the refrigerator door opening, realizing then that it was foolish to whisper, even as she understood the inclination. "Gab," she called again, this time putting all the energy she could into her voice so that Gabriella would hear her before replacing the milk in the fridge and leaving the apartment, taking all hope with her, hope for redemption to move this ton of a sin that covered her like a thousand sandbags. If not Gab, then who? By the time her roommates entered her room with that rubber band on her doorknob, she imagined the vultures would have already burst through the windows and eaten him to the bone, and she would have been picked alive, collateral damage. The image made her scream out. "Gab! Help me, please, Gab, help me."

She heard the apartment door close. Had Gabriella left? She stopped breathing, then her heart leapt as she heard feet shuffling, stopping at her door. "Cynt?"

"Help me, Gab, please open the door and come in and help me."

"You sure, I mean I'm seeing the rubber band—"

"Open the fucking door, Gab," she shouted.

"Well, damn, all right, girl," Gabriella said, and it seemed as if Gabriella took ten years to open the door as Cynthia watched the knob turn slowly, slowly; how long did it take to turn a knob to open a door? And then the rush of sound as Gabriella entered.

"Hit the light switch," Cynthia gasped.

"Where is it, it's too dark."

"Right there at eye level just inside the door."

Gabriella did and as soon as the light sprayed down from the ceiling Gabriella screamed and ran back out of the room and slammed the door shut, yelling, "What the hell, Cynthia? What, what, what the hell?"

"No, come back—"

"What? Why you tell me to open your door and turn on the light when you're like that? What the hell."

"Gab, please—"

"What in the ever-loving hell—"

"I can't move. Oh my god, I can't move."

"What? Well, tell him to get the hell off you."

"He can't."

"What?"

"He can't move."

"What?"

"I think he's dead—"

"What? Dead? Who?"

"It's him, Gab, from the lecture. Macon gave him my apartment number 'cause he thought that's where the get-together would be but I thought he wasn't comin' and then he did come and I thought it was Macon—"

"What? What the hell, Cynt?"

"Just come in here and help get him off me."

"What?"

"Stop saying *what* for god's sake."

"Wait, you're in there with a famous man like that, and you're saying he's dead and you're asking me to come help move him off you, and you're telling me to stop saying *what*? No. I will not stop saying *what*. Okay. What? What? What? What the ever-loving fuck, Cynthia. What?"

"Jesus, Gab, you gotta come in here to help me."

"Help you? Help you? I'll call 911. Okay. That will be my help. Okay."

"You cannot."

"You in no position to tell me what I cannot do. If he's dead, you have to call 911."

"But he might not be?"

"All the more reason."

"Can you just come in here and help me?"

"And do what?"

"Help me move him?"

"What?"

"We can call the police, okay? But at least let me, let me at least have on clothes. Please, Gab, please. Before Macon gets here."

"What?"

"He'll be here soon, I don't know when exactly—"

She stopped when she heard the door edge open. Gabriella walked in with one hand covering her eyes, the other extended to feel her way. "All right, tell me what to do, but make it quick."

"Can you, like, try to lift his head so I can at least move my shoulders and hoist up and then I get his arms from around me? If I can do that, I can get up."

"Where's his head?"

"Gab, you have to take your hand down so you can see."

"I will not, now where's his head?"

"Oh, Jesus, I never knew you to be so prudish—"

"Well, if not wanting to see this man naked, dead or alive, or you, makes me a prude, then I'm a prude—"

"You're gonna need both your hands, though."

Gabriella let out a huff of air as she took her hand down from her face. Her eyes were clamped shut, though, and she stretched her arms out in front of her as if she were blind. "Tell me something, where I am in here, 'cause if I go back out that door, I'm grabbing my shit and I'm back home."

"All right, you're, you know, at the top of the bed, but I'm thinking, you know, actually if you lift his legs that might even be better."

"What? Lift his legs? Lord, Cynt."

"Please." Cynthia's voice shook as she tried not to cry again. "Okay, well, then just his head. If you could just move his head. God, it's so heavy, his whole body is like crushing me. Please, Gab, you have to open your eyes."

"Where's a blanket or spread or quilt?"

Before Cynthia could say to look in the top of the closet, she heard the closet door crunch open, saw Gabriella pulling down the plush quilted spread Cynthia's grandmother had made for her. Red and blue, the school colors. Her grandmother was so proud of her, had poured her life into her. She thought about how devastated her grandmother would be over this. Would likely fault herself the way she knew deep down that her grandmother faulted herself for Cynthia's mother's behavior. She had to shut her thinking down about her grandmother right now, because it would make her too emotional and she'd be crying again, and right now she needed to call on her logic to help herself, and to keep Gabriella from hysteria.

Gabriella's hands shook as she spread the blanket over Cynthia and Mr. Z. Her glasses were crooked on her face and one eyebrow rose higher than the other as if to compensate. She leaned in and placed her finger on Mr. Z's neck, feeling for a pulse. "Lord have mercy," she said, her voice down to a whisper. "Nothing. He's not breathing."

"You sure?" Cynthia's voice shook.

"I'm pretty sure. How long has he been like this?"

"I fell asleep, I don't know, an hour, two?"

Gabriella leaned all the way over the bed to try to get to Mr. Z's head. "Damn, his head is all the way into the mattress."

"I know it is, that's one reason I can't move. You know, at first I thought he was . . . I don't know, resting?"

Gabriella managed to get her hands under his head to turn it around. She gasped and jumped back and covered her mouth to muffle her scream. "His eyes are wide open, Cynt, oh my God. The man is dead for real." She rushed her words then and jumped up and down. Cynthia started to wail. Despite her best efforts not to, she wailed as if her life was about to be over as she watched Gabriella backing toward the door.

"Where you going, Gab?" Cynthia asked. "Please don't leave me, Gab, please."

"I'm not leaving. How can I leave you? I should have never invited him over. I'm calling Mommy. She'll know what to do."

Eighteen

Cynthia thought she heard something as she sat by the pond with her face still buried in her arms, her arms still hugging her knees. She lifted her head. It was dark out now, but she was still warm, still dry, even as she sat on the ground, swaddled in Melanie's gift of the skiwear. In-ground lighting illuminated the pond and Cynthia could see where the ice had begun to crack. The cracks gave the pond an imperfection and also an impermanence that was comforting. Soon the ice would dissolve completely and the water would return to rippling and gurgling as it welcomed the overweight swan and the tadpoles and the guppies and the yellow-billed ducks and the imaginations of people like her who could sit and remember that evening when they saw themselves under a glaze of ice, cracking the freeze from the inside, breaking through. And it didn't even wreck her like she thought it would. Instead, she'd propelled herself along the wavy continuum toward accepting that she was neither victim nor villain that night. She was just a young woman, nineteen years old, testing the uncharted waters of her sensuality. She wasn't her mother, her vulnerable, mentally ill mother who had still managed to cobble together an atmosphere where Cynthia knew that she was loved. Her desire had skewed her judgment that night and that was her error. He hadn't turned around and left when he realized the display she was putting on wasn't for him; that was his failing. He manipulated her, he had. She'd been ripe for manipulation by believing that she was an ugly girl, and this fine man, this smart man, was making her feel beautiful.

"You never were ugly anyhow, girl," she said out loud and it seemed that she heard the cracks in the ice that glistened with possibility shout, *Hell no, you never were.*

Though what she heard wasn't coming from the pond as the sound formed into a recognizable shape as it moved through the cold. It was her name. She suddenly had the voice of her grandmother in her head when Rose would break out into singing the spiritual about hush, hush somebody's calling my name, oh my Lord, oh my Lord, who could it be. The somebodies calling her name were closer now and Cynthia put her arms around the impressive bark of the willow to stand, to turn around, and she heard squealing then. "There she is."

It was Tish and Lavia running down the path toward her, Tish in a full-length mink, Lavia more sensibly clothed in a puffer jacket.

"What the fuck, Cynthia, is your phone dead? We've been calling you, everybody's been. It's about Melanie," Tish shouted, frantically, waving her phone around.

"Melanie, oh dear god, is she okay, please Jesus, is she okay?" Cynthia said, as she put her hands on her head as if her world was about to crash in on her head. She started up the incline that led from the pond to get to them. The ground beneath her was slushy but also icy in spots and she skidded. She felt herself going down. *Not again!* she screamed in her head as the memory of falling down her double-wide staircase flashed through her brain. And she substituted the staircase for this scenario as she envisioned herself falling back into the cracked ice of the pond. She reached for a miracle the way she had reached for one that day on her staircase and her banister retreated and she'd pulled back air. There were no banisters here; she reached anyhow, expecting the same. But this time her miracle reached back as the air formed itself into hands, and she grabbed for them, and Tish and Lavia pulled her up the hill, holding on to her as she held on to them.

She was out of breath, the cold air exploding in her lungs. "Melanie, what, what about her?" she gasped.

"Here, sit," Lavia said, as they helped her to a bench and they flanked her as she sat.

"Tell me, tell me," she said, as she tried to catch her breath. Then Tish put her phone in Cynthia's hands.

"We're FaceTiming with E," Lavia said.

Cynthia held the phone in front of her. "E, E," she called. All she could see was a ceiling and a light. She could hear beeping then, people talking, fast. "Uh, uh, that's a hospital." She heard grunting then, crying out then. "Melanie, Melanie, dear god, Melanie's having the baby. E, E," she called again.

"Mom." She heard him before she could see him and then his face appeared, he had on a mask, scrubs, a cap. "Mom, Jesus, where the hell were you, I'm trying to help Melanie birth our baby and I have to worry about you, too."

"No, you don't have to worry about me, sweetheart—"

"The baby's coming early, Mom," he said and his voice shook and Cynthia realized that he was panicked not so much because he was *worried* about her, but because in this moment, he *needed* her.

"E, you listen to me, okay." She talked slowly, calmly. "That baby's coming here in the good Lord's time, not ours. Now, I want you to take some deep breaths, and then go help Melanie breathe. It's okay, and it's going to be okay. Now, you breathe. Let your breaths calm you. Are you hearing me?"

"Yes, okay, Mom. Okay," he said, as he pressed his eyes shut and Cynthia could see him taking in a deep breath. Then Emily, the doula, whom Cynthia met at one of the birthing classes she'd attended with Melanie, whispered in E's ear and he put the phone down and they were staring at the ceiling again, and listening to Melanie cry out, deep guttural cries.

Tish linked her arm in Cynthia's. "Whew, this some drama," Tish said.

"You were really good with E just then," Lavia said. "He was a mess when Tish reached him."

"He called the main number and got funneled to Antwon, who went to your cottage for a wellness check," Tish said, before Cynthia could ask what made her call E. "When you weren't there, Antwon came to my house looking for you, and we called E back who told us Melanie was soon to have the baby. I called him back just now to let him know you were okay when we saw you doing whatever you were doing. What the hell *were* you doing? You were supposed to be at my house two hours ago.

Walking around with a dead phone, you scared the shit out of us. Anyhow, I hit FaceTime by mistake when I was calling to tell E. So there you have it."

"Antwon went to get his searchlight," Lavia said, "and Tish was about to jump out of her skin so we just threw on our coats and started our own search."

"Must be nice to just throw on your coat and end up in that mink," Cynthia said to Tish.

"Oh yes, it's very nice," Tish said, as she unlinked her arm from Cynthia's and rubbed the sleeve along Cynthia's cheek. "You want to put it on, we could switch?"

"No, but I'll take a rain check for when I have somewhere fancy to go," Cynthia said.

"Girl, please, we got to create our own fancy. What's any fancier than waiting for my godchild to be born?"

Lavia laughed out loud and Cynthia did too, as she put her head on Tish's shoulder and rubbed the coat. And then she put her other arm around Tish and squeezed her so tightly as if she were saying, I'm so sorry about your dad.

Then they all sat up and moved in closer to the phone as they heard a voice say, "It's happening."

Someone was calling, numbers, BP, HR. Somebody else shouted, "Next push, Melanie, we're gonna get this baby out on the next push." Cynthia could barely make out E's voice above Melanie's earsplitting sobs, crying that she couldn't do it, it was too hard.

"Squeeze my hand, you can break it if you got to," E said.

And the doctor or the doula, Cynthia wasn't sure which, was

telling Melanie she'd already done it, one more push and the baby would be here.

Somebody propped up E's phone then; E would insist later that it wasn't him, nor the doula because she was at Melanie's side. Certainly not the obstetrician, or the pediatrician, or the nurse practitioner. Lavia said she was sure it was one of the people from environmental services who clean up the messes, because that's the type of thing her parents would have done, or her. "I would have done it without a second thought," she said.

Whoever propped the phone gave them a clear view to the baby crowning. Tish had her fists in her mouth and still her screaming sounds pushed past her fists and filled the night. Lavia had her fists under her chin; she wasn't screaming but her leg was bouncing up and down uncontrollably. Cynthia was motionless. She stared in the phone and willed the baby to come on. Melanie's crying seemed to pause suddenly for just a second that felt like everlasting. Then she let out a deep growl that sounded like it was coming from the bowels of the earth. And just like that, the doctor was holding the baby, glistening like a miracle, a slimy-mouth-stretched, crying-loud miracle.

"You got yourselves a girl, a beauty, too." And then the baby left their view.

"Why so quick, where are they taking her?" Tish asked as she sobbed on one side of Cynthia.

"A girl, a girl." Lavia was on the other side repeating, "Wow, wow, I think I peed myself."

Cynthia was still peering at the phone, showing the ceiling again. "Uh, please, Jesus," Cynthia said.

"What's happening?" Tish asked, her voice shaking. "Is everything okay?"

"They're weighing her?" Cynthia more asked than answered. "Doing the Apgar thing, you know, if she's 7 or higher that's good."

"Whoa, you got a five-pounder here," the doctor called.

"Yes!" E shouted.

"And she's a healthy 7," the doctor said.

Cynthia and Tish and Lavia jumped from the bench as if they were one person. They cheered and shouted, even Lavia shouted "Hallelujah!," accenting the word just like the holy women at Cynthia's grandmother's church. They barely heard E calling, saying, "Mom, it's a girl, five pounds and healthy, Mom," then E started to sob, a sound Cynthia could hear from a mile away so she picked up the phone.

Nineteen

On that night in 1975 Vince had just settled into his work-study shift at the high-rise dorm. He'd just returned from doing a stogie out back. He loved the midnight to eight because he could get high on the clock and still earn the 20 percent differential as he laughed, dozed, and munched the night away. He rarely insisted that anybody sign in, as if this were a freshman dorm. And after a month into the semester he mostly knew the residents and their regular visitors anyhow.

But his high was blown the night the uncles showed up— Nathan the detective, Hal the preacher, and Don the bartender. After the Black students arrived in droves, and left in scatters, which he was generally cool with—he considered himself a down white boy, and as a scholarship recipient he identified with the Black students' insistence that they had as much right to surf this Ivy League ocean as anyone else—he leaned back in the swivel chair, his feet on the desk, sipped his cherry Coke, and commenced to solve the cryptogram in the *Evening Bulletin*.

Then the triplets stormed the door like gangbusters. They weren't really triplets, but that's the name he gave the uncles in his head because they looked so much alike. Three Black men, early forties, which was senior citizen status to his nineteen-year-old self. All three walked with the jaunty hipness of the men in *Shaft* or *Super Fly*. They had big Afros and big attitudes that signaled *fuck with me at your peril.*

He sat up with a start as they approached the desk, even before Nathan, the police detective, called out, "Yo, Blue Blood," and then flashed a police badge. Vince tilted the cherry Coke he'd been sipping and watched in weed-induced confusion as the red-brown liquid spilled onto the desk. "Whoa, shit, sorry," he said, as he wiped up the spill with the hem of his KEEP ON TRUCKING T-shirt. "Uh, can I help you, sir? Uh, sirs?"

"What's your name, Blue Blood?" Nathan asked.

"Uh, it's Vince, and can I just say that I'm nobody's blue blood. With respect, I say that, of course."

"That so?" Nathan said, as he scanned the clipboard on the ledge next to the desk where Vince stood. "Well, if your blood is as red as your eyes, damn, what you been smoking? And I don't ask that in my official capacity, though we could make it official depending on you."

"Uh, sir?" Vince said.

"Leave the kid alone, Detective," Hal, the preacher, said.

"Forgive our friend here," Don, the bartender, said, nodding his head at Nathan. "He just gets antsy this time of night. He's just here because he got a call from his baby brother who goes to community college and tried to party over here with the rich kids and tied one on and got sloppy drunk and now needs help getting home."

Nathan lowered his head and shook it back and forth, feigning embarrassment. "The last time, I had to sling him over my shoulder and carry him to my car. Let's hope he can leave here upright tonight."

"Uh, sure, if I can do anything—" Vince said.

"You know, Vince," Nathan said, as if the thought had just occurred to him, "we gonna pull the car around back, so if you could disarm that back door there so the alarm doesn't wake the dead, you'd be doing a public service."

"Oh, it's already off," Vince said, then added quickly that he would recheck to make sure.

He breathed a sigh of relief later when he heard them arguing as they got off the elevator. Heard the one telling the obviously drunk one that he was killing their mother with this getting drunk shit every night. Vince started to get up and walk around the corner to the hallway that led to the elevator. He decided against it, glad that they weren't there for anything more serious. Anything more serious and he would have had to alert the building administrators. And all he wanted to do was finish his cryptogram and groove on his high.

· · ·

After Hal had prayed over the body and Nathan asked Cynthia was she all right, had she been hurt in any way, and Don made tea for Cynthia and Gabriella, the uncles went into the back bedroom and argued over where to take him.

Hal said they should report it for it was "old-ass man tried to party in a young girl's room and had a heart attack."

"Yeah, but then Cynthia's got to live that," Don said. "They might kick her out of school and she's months from her degree."

"She's gonna have to live with it regardless," Hal said, "but I agree; no sense in having her reputation sullied like that for the world to know."

"I say we leave him in the dumpster like the trash that he is," Nathan said. "I mean, got damn, I read his books and shit, and his pastime is trying to get in young girls' dorm beds."

They went back and forth until they agreed they'd been in the building for too long, and they needed to do something quick.

"What about Clara?" Don said.

"Clara, yeah, you a fucking genius, man," Nathan said.

"Okay, I'm following you, Clara's," Hal said, "though remember Mom said I'm the smartest and that don't change."

They all knew Clara. She ran a gentlemen's club from her house. It was a decent house and she protected the women she employed and screened her clients to keep them safe. She went to Hal's church every Sunday and insisted that the women who worked for her did the same. Nathan looked out for her, Hal prayed with her, and Don referred his bar patrons to her if they passed his muster.

They agreed that Gordon Willis should have gone to Clara's tonight instead of dying in Cynthia's bed. Nathan came back into the living room and asked to use the phone. Cynthia nodded, dazed. And Gabriella asked what the plan was. He told them they would handle it. "That guy in there never showed up for the party. That's all you got to remember. And he damned sure didn't show up here."

Nathan called Clara as Hal prayed with Cynthia and Gabriella. He told them afterward that whatever the next thing they planned to do had this not happened, do that thing. So Cynthia took the long walk to her grandmother's, stopping at the deli along the way. She thought that the cleaning of the chandelier, her mother's instincts to suggest it, saved her that day.

Twenty

The first few times it was awkward for them. Bloc kept dropping his weed pipe, Tish kept spilling her wine, twice Cynthia had to leave early because of dizzy spells when it hit her that Gordon Willis was Tish's father. Though an acceptance was also settling in, and she could say his real name in her head, and to Gabriella, and her breath didn't catch in her throat. Lavia was the steadying force though, quick-wittedly snarky enough to settle them down. They managed to recapture the sense of merriment they'd discovered when they'd gathered at Tish's when Cynthia first moved in. Now, though, there was the dimension of real truth-telling when Lavia could reference her childhood on the cruise ship, Bloc could talk about that beautiful lab Shelly, and how she brought him back from the brink. Cynthia was freed up to talk about her college years, knowing there was just one night that was taboo, just one night, not her entire undergraduate time. And Tish, Tish being Tish, chose a larger stage for her embrace of the truth.

It was the champagne brunch to welcome the new residents. But not the regular brunch that had winnowed down to every few months because just about all the cottages had been sold. This one was an annual celebration that included families and friends. This one was held in the grand ballroom with light shimmering from not one but four chandeliers. Cynthia sat at the table with Tish and Tish's cousin GG. Bloc and his daughter and grandchildren arrived. Bloc leaned in and kissed Cynthia's lips, and his daughter asked if Melanie was coming; they'd discovered they were in the same sorority when they'd gotten together the month before.

"Yes, she and E are coming," Cynthia said, "but you know with a six-month-old they're always running late."

"As long as they're bringing my godchild," Tish said.

"Cynthia, I have tried to explain to Tish that she has to be asked, she can't just appoint herself godmother," GG said to laughter.

"Are there enough seats?" Bloc asked. "We can find another table if not."

"No, no, no," Tish said, as she jumped up. "We can grab another chair or two. I'll be making an announcement shortly, and I want the people closest to me to be where I can see them. Where the heck is Lavia?"

"I saw her when I came in, looked to be with a tall, good-looking white guy," GG said.

Tish tilted her head. "Lavia?" she said.

"Yes, Lavia." Lavia came up behind Tish's chair, and Tish sat back, way back to take in the sight of Lavia and Robert.

"Well, well, well, and who do we have here? Might you be a new resident?" Tish asked.

"Not yet, but that's my goal," he said, as he squeezed the back of Lavia's neck and Lavia introduced him around the table.

Roy, the new head of the residents association, was on the stage making opening remarks, and then he said that he wanted to introduce a special resident, and he had no idea what she wanted to say. "But I'm sure it will be, well, special." Ripples of laughter spread through the room.

Tish took center stage dressed like the room she was in, a tailored taffeta pantsuit, the color of honey. She looked nervous and Cynthia wondered what she was about to say. "I first want to make an announcement that I'm available," she said, to up-roarious laughter.

"Lord have mercy on my cousin," GG said, as she shook her head. "She can't help it."

"Next I want to say that I'm reclaiming my name," Tish said, and GG gasped as her eyes filled with tears. "I changed my name because I was ashamed of my father, the way he died."

E and Melanie walked into the ballroom then, and Tish interrupted herself to say, "Oh, there's my goddaughter," and a chorus of oohs and ahs ushered E and Melanie and the baby to the table and Cynthia had her hand out, ready to grab her grandchild just as Tish was saying out loud her reclaimed name, Natasha Willis, the daughter of Dr. Gordon Willis. GG stood and applauded, saying "Yes, yes!" Other people joined in; many stood as well, white people not sure why, but standing anyhow and applauding, thinking this must be a Black thing, so okay.

Bloc looked confused; Lavia and Robert, trained spies that they were, sat expressionless. And Cynthia did what Gabriella's uncle had suggested she do years ago. *Whatever the next thing is you were about to do before that thing that happened, happened, do that next thing.*

Cynthia had her hands out ready to grab the baby when Tish made her proclamation. She did her next thing; she took the baby in her arms and squeezed her. She sat her in her lap and swayed. Tish returned to the table, and Tish and GG hugged and cried.

"That's really something you just did there, Tish," Lavia said when Tish had settled down.

"It was," Bloc said, "and I'm not even sure what just happened."

"She just stood in her truth, wow," Cynthia said, as she swayed the baby side to side, grateful that Gabriella had prepared her.

"Some truths are meant to be told to a ballroom filled with people, and other truths are meant to be whispered to the wind alone," Lavia said, as she looked at Cynthia and winked. And Cynthia was sure that Lavia knew. "And I guess it takes living at a place called the Sexagenarian, Gen for short, to figure out the difference."

Cynthia nodded and kissed the top of her grandbaby's head. She thought about how'd she'd tell Tish that she'd heard Gordon Willis give a talk at Penn, that he was a phenomenal speaker. That's all she'd say. She breathed in the air that smelled of teak and new life coming. Even at this age, new life coming.

Acknowledgments

Each novel is a journey, and I'm so grateful for the people who rode with me for *Our Gen*: Suzanne Gluck, my tenacious agent, is better than a GPS for charting a course through the fog that led me to a new home at Amistad and a writer's dream of an editor, the insightful Patrik Bass, along with his assistant, Francesca Walker; my family of early readers and listeners including James Rahn of Rittenhouse Writers'; my real family—sisters Paula, Gwen, Elaine, Vernell, and niece-sisters Robin and Celeste; my children Taiwo and Kehinde, and my other two, their spouses Aaron and Teresa; the grandchildren Kennedy, Josephine, Ryan, and Michael, whose smiles confirm that there is a God; and always, always Greg.

About the Author

Author of the critically acclaimed novels *Tumbling*, *Tempest Rising*, *Blues Dancing*, *Leaving Cecil Street*, *Trading Dreams at Midnight*, and *Lazaretto*, Diane McKinney-Whetstone is the recipient of numerous awards, including the Black Caucus of the American Library Association's Literary Award for Fiction, which she won twice. She lives in Philadelphia with her husband, Greg.